Helen Paiba is known as one of the most committed, knowledgeable and acclaimed children's booksellers in Britain. For more than twenty years she owned and ran the Children's Bookshop in Muswell Hill, London, which under her guidance gained a superb reputation for its range of children's books and for the advice available to its customers.

Helen was involved with the Booksellers Association for many years and served on both its Children's Bookselling Group and the Trade Practices Committee. In 1995 she was given honorary life membership of the Booksellers Association of Great Britain and Ireland in recognition of her outstanding services to the association and to the book trade. In the same year the Children's Book Circle (sponsored by Books for Children) honoured her with the Eleanor Farjeon Award, given for distinguished service to the world of children's books.

She retired in 1995 and now lives in London.

Adventure

STORIES

for Seven Year Olds

COMPILED BY HELEN PAIBA

ILLUSTRATED BY MARK SOUTHGATE

MACMILLAN
CHILDREN'S BOOKS

For the Kennard children in Manchester with love HP

First published 2000 by Macmillan Children's Books
a division of Macmillan Publishers Limited
20 New Wharf Road, London N1 9RR
Basingstoke and Oxford
www.panmacmillan.com

Associated companies throughout the world

ISBN 0 330 39139 9

A CIP catalogue record for this book is available from
the British Library.

Typeset by SX Composing DTP, Rayleigh, Essex
Printed and bound in Great Britain by
Mackays of Chatham plc, Kent

Contents

The Horrible Holiday Treasure Hunt

Margaret Mahy

It was holiday time in Ditchwater.

"*We're* going camping at the beach," boasted Allan.

"*We're* taking off for the city," said Phoebe, dancing. "My mum says we'll shop till we drop. What are *you* going to do, Rowan?"

She knew exactly what Rowan was going to do, but she wanted to make her say it aloud.

"Go to the library, I suppose," said Rowan. "I have to stay in Ditchwater, because Mum and Dad are both working."

"*Boring*!" said Allan.

"But I *like* reading," said Rowan quickly.

"I don't," said Phoebe. "Libraries are dull –

dull as Ditchwater!" she added with a laugh. "Never mind! We'll send you postcards, telling you what a great time we're having."

(Of course if Phoebe had been a reader, she would have known that ditchwater is often the liveliest sort of water there is, full of parties and processions, though you only see them by looking through a microscope.)

Anyhow, off went all the holiday children – Phoebe and Allan of course, along with Davy, Marvin, Selina, Phoenix, Eudora, Bella and Richard, while Rowan's parents worked hard, trying to pay off their mortgage. Rowan began her holidays by visiting the library where her uncle Torrance worked as Children's Librarian.

"I'd love to put on special holiday programmes," sighed Uncle Torrance, "but the library just doesn't have enough money for them these days. This new library manager the council has appointed is dreadfully stern about finance, and I have to work from early in the morning until late at night just to keep the library going. I used to have time to read and garden, but now my garden is such a jungle that I have lost my zinnias and I'm frightened to walk up my own path in case maddened elephants charge out of the woods. As for reading, I haven't had time to read for ages."

He cast a longing eye at a big blue book called *The Alligator's Garden*, which had just been beautifully rebound by the library bindery. Though librarians are forbidden to read while at work, Uncle Torrance couldn't resist flipping *The Alligator's Garden* open at page one while pretending to pay attention to the computer in front of him.

But, before he could read a single word, a ferocious shadow fell across page one. A huge, hairy man with a patch over one eye, a parrot on his shoulder and a pistol in his belt was looming over them. Fortunately librarians are very brave. (Not a lot of people know this.)

"Can I help you?" Uncle Torrance asked in a kindly librarianish way.

"I do hope so – for your sake, shipmate," snarled the hairy one. "I am Hebhole, but you may call me 'Horrible'."

"Horrible! Horrible!" shouted the parrot gleefully. Hebhole thumped the issue desk.

"Now listen here, matey," he cried. "I have a problem. My old aunt, who was a pirate like me, died only this morning. '*Horrible*,' she said with her dying breath (for friends and family *all* call me by my first name), '*let me whisper a secret. I was once a member of the Ditchwater Civic Library, and of course that meant getting my library books back on time which can be a problem for a pirate. I would sail secretly up the Ditchwater River, and slide slyly into the library. And then, after changing my library books, I would treat myself to a hamburger.*

'*But one day, while I was deciding between double cheese or triple beef-with-bacon, police cars came screaming up the main street, all pointing straight at me. I had been betrayed by my bo'sun, and I was forced to leap walls, hide under hedges, scramble through drainpipes and so on. Of course I was carrying my treasure with me (no use leaving treasure on board when your bo'sun is unreliable), and it certainly did weigh me down. So I buried that* treasure under a lot of zinnias in someone's front garden, and then I hastily scrawled a treasure map in one of my library books . . . a red-covered one (though of course I am strongly opposed to drawing in library books, and if I caught any of my crew doing such a thing, I would make them walk the plank).

'Back to my ship I ran, moving very nimbly now I had nothing to carry but library books. Horrakapotchkin! My ship had disappeared (did I mention I had a treacherous bo'sun?) and the police were waiting on the wharf. They snatched my library books (though those books were not due back for another three weeks), and clapped me in a prison cell. Fortunately I had a file hidden in a false compartment in my wooden leg. Within seconds, I'd filed through the bars on my cell window, stolen a police boat and set off after that bo'sun. I never dared return to Ditchwater, but if anyone else had found that map in the red-covered book it would have been the main item on the television news. So somewhere on the shelves of Ditchwater Library there is an unknown library book with my treasure map in it.' And here my aunt paused to suck in another dying breath . . .

'What was the title of that red-covered book?' I asked, deeply fascinated by her tale.

'*That red-covered book was called* . . .' she mumbled. '*That book was called . . . Arrrrrrgh!*'"

"Oh, we don't have that book in the library," Uncle Torrance interrupted, shaking his head. "I would remember a title like that."

"That wasn't the title, shipmate," shouted Horrible. "That was the great groan my aunt groaned as she gave up the ghost. Leaving her funeral arrangements to others, I hastened to join the Ditchwater library, and have been given an official Ditchwater library card with my name on it. So – bring me that book with the red cover!"

"We do have rather *a lot* of books with red covers," said Uncle Torrance doubtfully. "Didn't your aunt give you any other clue?"

"If she'd lived ten seconds longer I would have known every single thing about that book," growled Hebhole sourly. "But she didn't, so I don't. You're the librarian! Find it quickly!"

"You must put in a request," said Uncle Torrance. "I'll do what I can."

"You'd better," hissed Hebhole. "Make sure that book is here when I call in next week, for disappointment brings out the worst in me."

"The worst! The worst!" shouted the parrot as Horrible Hebhole stumped away.

"A red-covered book," Uncle Torrance sighed, looking doubtfully at the shelves.

But Rowan leaped up, glowing with excitement.

"A treasure hunt!" she cried. "I'll find all the other kids who haven't gone away for the holidays, and we'll search every red cover in the library."

Off she ran, but ten minutes later she was back again followed by Dora, Maurice, Handley, Marla, Lily, Kevin, Bernice, Stephanie, Max, Ginsberg, Oliver, Rosie and a whole lot of other children, all of whom had library cards and working parents. Choosing whole armfuls of books with red covers, they carried them into the Ditchwater park and began searching through them.

Postcards from Allen and Phoebe arrived at the library. It seemed there were bus strikes in the city and thunderstorms at the beach. However, the left-behind holiday children were far too busy to feel sorry for absent friends. For Ditchwater was no longer dull. All around the park and the playground, up and down the footpaths, sat groups of children, surrounded by tottering towers of red-covered books, all eager to find Horrible's treasure map.

At first the search was speedy and straight-forward, but almost at once difficulties arose. For, as they searched, the children couldn't help catching a glimpse of a word here or a word there, and of course once you have read one word it is hard not to read the word that comes after it. Before you know it, you find you have read a whole line without meaning to. And once you have read a whole line it is hard not to take an interest in the line below. So many of the children found themselves actually reading the stories in the red-covered books, and becoming so interested in those stories that the books were thoroughly read inside as well as out.

A week later Horrible Hebhole came stumping back into town. His parrot looked around then screamed "Wrong town! Wrong town!" and no wonder. Everyone in Ditchwater was having such a wonderful time. People on park benches, boys and girls at bus stops were busily searching through red-covered books, then crying "Listen to this!" and reading one another exciting bits they had unexpectedly come across.

"You'll never find the treasure map if you waste time reading," Hebhole heard a big brother say to his little sister as they sat searching under a tree.

"But isn't the story a sort of treasure?" asked the little sister.

"Let me see!" shouted Horrible Hebhole, leaning over the hedge and snatching the book, in case the sister (being little) had found the treasure map without quite realizing it. However, there was nothing but print on the page. Hebhole sighed, and tossed the book back to her. She began reading once more . . . reading aloud too.

". . . Hugo stood in the doorway, looking into darkness. Suddenly yellow talons swooped out of the shadows behind him and clawed at his shoulder."

The little sister fell silent.

"Go on! Go on!" screamed Hebhole's parrot.

"Yes, go on," shouted Hebhole. "What happened next?" The little sister was forced to read right to the very end of the book, with the parrot shouting "Don't stop!" whenever she paused to take a breath.

"Well, there's no treasure map in *that* book, my hearties," said Horrible Hebhole. "On to the next one! What's it called?"

"*The Ghastly Mystery of the Haunted Eggbeater*," said the little sister.

"Don't stop," cried the parrot.

"No! Don't!" agreed Hebhole, settling himself to listen to the next red-covered story.

Meanwhile, Uncle Torrance actually found himself with time on his hands, for it was now Rowan who programmed the library computers to locate all books with red covers, while her Ditchwater friends jogged in and out of the library, either borrowing or returning red-cover collections. The children's library's holiday issues soared like eagles. Of course Uncle Torrance should have gone home early and struggled with his jungle. He might even have located his zinnias. But . . . "First things first," he muttered to himself, and he stayed in the library, reading *The Alligator's Garden*, his head filled with wild visions of dancing alligators.

"Listen!" cried Rowan suddenly. "Stamping feet! It must be Hebhole."

However, it wasn't Hebhole (who was sitting in the park, listening to a horror story called *The Vampire Teddy Bear*). It was Ignatius Croop, the library manager. He had never so much as set foot in a children's library before, and, just for a moment, he was confounded by its colour and cacophony. However, he quickly recovered.

"What *is* going on here?" he cried. "Children are taking out hundreds of red-covered books. If this goes on the council will start taking books seriously once more."

"And why not?" asked Uncle Torrance, rapidly sitting on *The Alligator's Garden* so that Ignatius would not see that he had been reading himself.

"How can I convince the councillors to upgrade the computer system if boys and girls are borrowing books?" shouted Ignatius indignantly. "What *is* going on?"

"We're searching for a lost treasure map which a pirate queen hid in a red-covered library book," explained Rowan boldly.

"Treasure? Emeralds maybe? Or diamonds?" gasped Ignatius Croop. His eyes glittered with greed. "Why, if we found pirate treasure we could probably buy a whole system of mainframe computers, and people would get their questions answered before they even knew what they were." (And I could ask the council for a bonus, he was thinking, though he did not say this aloud.) "Let's get this search properly organized," he shouted. "No more taking books out of the library! And no more *reading*," he added.

All working parents were pleased to think that their little ones were being looked after at the library – a very reliable institution. And soon, not only children and librarians but city councillors too, found themselves picking up red-covered books from the left, flicking through the pages, then placing them in piles on the right while Ignatius Croop strode up and down shouting "Faster! Faster!" It was amazing what you could find nestling between the pages . . . book marks and four-leafed clovers of course, along with bills, love letters, photographs, pressed flowers, dog collars, articles torn from newspapers, lost spectacles, postcards explaining that it was raining at the seaside, a slice of bacon that some vandal had used as a bookmark, half a pair of false teeth, recipes for delicious cakes, hair ribbons and so on. But no treasure maps!

"Faster! Faster!" howled Ignatius, prowling past teams of searchers. "It *must* be there somewhere."

"Oh, I don't know if employing a library manager was a good idea after all," moaned the councillors. Their fingers were sore and swollen from shaking red-covered books – and all in vain.

Suddenly the library door burst open. There was the sound of a parrot imitating a trumpet call. Then in swept that parrot, poised on the shoulder of a person with a patch and a pistol.

"No parrots in the library," shouted Ignatius. "If parrot mites get in the computers I will not be responsible."

"Avast there, matey!" cried Horrible Hebhole – for it was indeed he – "What has happened to the supply of red-covered books?"

Ignatius gave a servile smile.

"We're doing our best to locate the treasure map—" he began.

"Horrakapotchin!" shrieked Horrible Hebhole. "Forget the treasure map. *What has happened to my stories?*"

"The library is not here to provide stories," Ignatius declared loftily. "And red-covered books are not to be taken from library premises."

"But, shipmate," said Hebhole in a sinister voice, "I have a library card."

By now all the searchers were listening to the argument with deep interest . . . all except Uncle Torrance who thought he might dip into *The Alligator's Garden*. If this argument proved to be a long one, he might have time to read all the next chapter. He opened his book quickly – then leaped to his feet, exclaiming in horror.

"Some fiend has scribbled on page sixty-one," he bellowed.

"Another word from you about *charging* for library services and I'll *puncture* you," Hebhole was yelling at Ignatius Croop. But Rowan shouted louder than either of them.

"Uncle! That's not a scribble. That's a treasure map."

Horrible Hebhole snatched up *The Alligator's Garden*. His one eye nearly leaped from his head, and even his patch flapped like a flag in a gale.

"It *is*, it *is*!" he shouted. "Blessings on the Ditchwater children's library."

He did not notice Ignatius Croop seizing a copy of *Webster's Dictionary*, planning to stun Hebhole and to snatch the treasure map

himself. However, because of carrying piles of books around day after day, librarians are very strong. (Not a lot of people know this.) Uncle Torrance leaped in front of Hebhole, seized Ignatius, whirled him round a few times then flung him in a nor-easterly direction. Ignatius flew like a bullet into the Reference section, where he struck an old-fashioned catalogue cabinet and collapsed in a heap. Uncle Torrance turned to Hebhole, looking bewildered.

"It just cannot be," he said. "*The*

Alligator's Garden is a book with a *blue* cover."

"But *The Alligator's Garden* had just come back from the bindery," called Rowan excitedly. "It must have been given a new blue cover. Anyhow we've found the map, and that's all that matters."

"And I can see what a good thing it is to know more about a book than the colour of its cover," said Hebhole in a particularly sincere voice for a pirate. "And I must say that, since listening to the red-covered stories children have been reading me, I am a changed man and my parrot is a changed parrot. But first things first. Does anyone in the library have a spade?"

Imagine Uncle Torrance's astonishment when the treasure hunters (children and councillors mixed together, all armed with spades borrowed from the Parks and Reserves Division) joined together into a great treasure-seeking gang and faithfully followed the map, street by street, to his very own jungle. Within an hour they had pulled out every weed, constructed a useful compost heap and had sorted the horse-radish from the hollyhocks. And towards the end of the day, as sunset bathed them all in a golden glow, the parrot let out a scream of triumph. Hebhole had found the lost zinnias. Carefully he began digging between them. And there it was! The treasure chest at last! Like a true pirate Hebhole fell on his knees beside it and tore it open. Diamonds, rubies and emeralds tumbled in a glittering stream among the zinnias.

"Treasure! Treasure," shouted the parrot. Hebhole rose to his feet.

"In the beginning I was planning to keep this treasure all to myself," he said, "but listening to those stories has reformed me. Now I plan to donate every diamond – every emerald – to the Children's Library, provided the treasure is entirely devoted to the purchase of good books, red-covered whenever possible."

Councillors and children cheered so loudly that, over in the library, Ignatius Croop heard their triumphant ululation. He immediately packed his cell-phone and set off for the wharf. What happened to him after that I cannot say, but Hebhole's pirate ship certainly vanished, and the Councillors, since they were forced to appoint a new library manager, quickly gave him Croop's job. As you have probably guessed, Hebhole couldn't actually read, but the parrot could, and it worked out well, for Hebhole, in return for having *The Alligator's Garden* read aloud to him in the evenings, did everything Uncle Torrance told him to.

And when Allan and Phoebe came home from their holidays and realized what they had missed out on – well, they both rushed out to join the library at once and managed to become good readers themselves, though never quite as good as Rowan and certainly never as good as Hebhole's parrot, who, after listening eagerly to many good stories rose, in due course, to the rank of city librarian.

Playing with Cuthbert

René Goscinny

I wanted to go out and play with our gang, but Mum said no, nothing doing, she didn't care for the little boys I went around with, we were always up to something silly, and anyway I was invited to tea with Cuthbert, who was a nice little boy with such good manners, and it would be a very good thing if I tried to be more like him.

I wasn't mad keen to go to tea with Cuthbert, or try to be more like him. Cuthbert is top of the class and teacher's pet and a rotten sport but we can't thump him much because of his glasses. I'd rather have gone to the swimming pool with Alec and Geoffrey and Eddie and the rest, but there it was, Mum looked as if she wasn't standing for any nonsense, and anyway I always do what my mum says, especially when she looks as if she isn't standing for any nonsense.

Mum made me wash and comb my hair and told me to put on my blue sailor suit with the nice creases in the trousers, and my white silk shirt and spotted tie. I had to wear that lot for my cousin Angela's wedding, the time I was sick after the reception.

"And don't look like that!" said Mum. "You'll have a very nice time playing with Cuthbert, I'm sure."

Then we went out. I was scared stiff of meeting the gang. They'd have laughed like a drain to see me got up like that!

Cuthbert's mum opened the door. "Oh, isn't he sweet!" she said, and she hugged me and then she called Cuthbert. "Cuthbert! Come along. Here's your little friend Nicholas." So Cuthbert came along, he was all dressed up too, with velvet trousers and white socks and funny shiny black sandals. We looked a pair of right Charlies, him and me.

Cuthbert didn't look all that pleased to see me either, he shook my hand and his hand was all limp. "Well, I'll be off," said Mum. "I hope he'll behave, and I'll be back to pick him up at six." And Cuthbert's mum said she was sure we'd play nicely and I'd be very good. Mum gave me a rather worried look and then she went away.

We had tea. That was OK, there was chocolate to drink and jam and cake and biscuits and we didn't put our elbows on the table. After tea Cuthbert's mum told us to go and have a nice game in Cuthbert's room.

Up in his room Cuthbert started by telling me I mustn't thump him because he wore glasses and if I did he'd start to shout and his mum would have me put in prison. I told him I'd just love to thump him, but I wasn't going to because I'd promised my mum to be good. Cuthbert seemed to like the sound of that, and he said right, we'd play. He got out heaps of books: geography books and science books and arithmetic books, and he said we could read and do some sums to pass the time. He told me he knew some brilliant problems about the water from taps running into a bath with the plug pulled out so the bath emptied at the same time as it was filling.

That didn't sound like a bad idea, and I asked Cuthbert if I could see his bath because it might be fun. Cuthbert looked at me, took off his glasses, wiped them, thought a minute and then told me to come with him.

There was a big bath in the bathroom and I said why didn't we fill it and sail boats on it? Cuthbert said he'd never thought of that, but it was quite a good idea. The bath didn't take long to fill right up to the top (we put the plug in, not like the problem). But then we were stuck because Cuthbert didn't have any boats to sail in it. He explained that he didn't have many toys at all, he mostly had books. But luckily I can make paper boats and we took some pages out of his arithmetic book. Of course we tried to be careful so that Cuthbert could stick the pages back in the book afterwards, because it's very naughty to harm a book, a tree or a poor dumb animal.

We had a really great time. Cuthbert swished his arm about in the water to make waves. It was a pity he didn't roll up his shirt-sleeves first, and he didn't take off the watch he got for coming first in the last history test we had and now it says twenty past four all the time. After a bit longer, I don't know just how much longer because of the watch not working, we'd had enough of playing boats. Anyway there was water all over the place and we didn't want to make too much mess because there were muddy puddles on the floor and Cuthbert's sandals weren't as shiny as they used to be.

We went back to Cuthbert's room and he

showed me his globe, which is a big metal ball on a stand with seas and continents and things on it. Cuthbert explained that it was for learning geography and finding where the different countries were. I knew that already, there's a globe like that at school and our teacher showed us how it works. Cuthbert told me you could unscrew his globe, and then it was like a big ball. I think it was me that got the idea of playing ball with it, only that turned out not to be such a very good idea after all. We did have some fun throwing and catching the globe, but Cuthbert had taken off his glasses so as not to risk breaking them, and he doesn't see very well without his glasses, so he missed the globe and the part with Australia on it hit his mirror and the mirror got broken. Cuthbert put his glasses on again to see what had happened and he was very upset. We put the globe back on its stand and decided to be more careful in case our mums weren't too pleased.

So we looked for something else to do, and Cuthbert told me his dad had given him a chemistry set to help him with science. He showed me the chemistry set; it's brilliant. It's a big box full of tubes and funny round bottles and little flasks full of things all different colours, and a spirit burner too. Cuthbert told me you could do some very instructive experiments with this chemistry set.

He started pouring little bits of powder and liquid into the tubes and they changed colour and went red or blue and now and then there was a puff of white smoke. It was ever so instructive. I told Cuthbert we ought to try something even more instructive, and he agreed. We took the biggest bottle and tipped all the powders and liquids into it and then we got the spirit burner and heated up the bottle. It was OK to start with; the stuff began frothing up, and then there was some very black smoke. The trouble was the smoke didn't smell too good and it made everything very dirty. When the bottle burst we had to stop the experiment.

Cuthbert started howling that he couldn't see any more, but luckily it was only because the lenses of his glasses were all black, and while he wiped them I opened the window, because the smoke was making us cough. And the froth was making funny noises on the carpet, like boiling water, and the walls were all black and we weren't terribly clean ourselves.

Then Cuthbert's mum came in. For a moment she didn't say anything at all, just opened her eyes and her mouth very wide, and then she started to shout, she took off Cuthbert's glasses and then she led us off

to the bathroom to get washed. When Cuthbert's mum saw the bathroom she wasn't too pleased about that either.

Cuthbert's mum went off, telling me she was going to ring my mother and ask her to come and fetch me immediately and she'd never seen anything like it in all her born days and it was absolutely incredible.

Mum did come to fetch me pretty soon, and I was pleased because I wasn't having so much fun at Cuthbert's house any more, not with his mum carrying on like that. Mum took me home, telling me all the way she supposed I was proud of myself and I wouldn't have any pudding this evening. I must say, that was fair enough, because we did do one or two daft things at Cuthbert's. And actually Mum was right, as usual: I *did* have a nice time playing with Cuthbert. I'd have liked to go and see him again, but it seems that Cuthbert's mum doesn't want him to be friends with me.

Honestly, mothers! I do wish they could make up their minds, you just don't know *who* to play with!

Horatio the Jellyfish

Anna Fienberg

"**Y**ou're a drifter at heart," the jellyfish told her son fondly. "Just like your dear father before you."

"What happened to *his* father before *him*?" said young Horatio Jellyfish, who liked to set things straight.

"He tended to get stuck in seaweed, and was eaten by an eyeless violet sea snail," said his mother. "So let that be a warning to you, my darling: drift far but cautiously, on the great sea of life."

She was about to say more when a wave from the great sea of life lifted her up and away, and the two were separated for ever.

"Mamma!" called Horatio Jellyfish. "Mamma, come back!" But only the slippery slap of the sea echoed his lonely cry.

Horatio shivered. He stared at the empty ocean, and his heart plunged to the tip of his tentacles. How could he go on drifting without his mother? She had been the only anchor in his life, the one thing he could count on. She was the one who had warned him about the deadly Pufferfish and the stinging coral, not to mention the terrible Sea Witch who kept eels in her boots. Yes, his mamma had always been there, clutching his little tentacles tightly in her own.

Horatio floated sadly on. He passed blue sea stars and angelfish the colour of the sun. Coral shrimps called out good morning, and butterfly fish freckled the waves. But Horatio saw nothing.

Only the memory of his mother trembled before his eyes.

Horatio drifted like this for twenty-three days. Occasionally he would have a word with a sea urchin or fill in a minute or two with a fairy basslet, but as soon as the conversation grew interesting, the current would tug him, and away he floated.

That was the trouble with being a wanderer, thought Horatio Jellyfish. You may travel and see the world, but you could lose your mother, and you never had a conversation lasting more than a wavelength. You could never hang around long enough to make a friend.

"I may be a drifter at heart," he told a banana fish as he passed by, "just like my father before me, but what I'd really like is to have a good rest on a rock and a decent chinwag with someone."

Horatio was drifting past a forest of red coral when something unusual caught his eye. Down below he saw a golden light shining. It lit up the water so that he could see cuttlefish changing colour for dinner, and sea horses swapping their news.

On all his travels, Horatio had never seen anything as beautiful as this light. The current pushed him along, closer and closer, until he was floating right up to the centre of the light. It streamed from the window of a large conch shell, and now he could hear an enchanting song coming from inside.

A mermaid with wild yellow hair opened the door and saw Horatio drifting by. Suddenly he was bathed in golden light so that his tentacles shone like Christmas ribbon. Madeline the mermaid nodded in her friendly way, but continued to sing as if her life depended on it.

"Hello, my friend," she sang in F major, "pardon me if I sing so loudly, but my voice is my only defence."

"Defence?" asked Horatio. "Defence against what . . . or whom?"

How could the owner of such a magnificent, miraculous, melodious voice ever have an enemy?

But just then the great sea of life heaved again and Horatio drifted helplessly away.

"*Always* interrupted!" he exploded. "Never hear *anything* to the end." And he shook his tentacles in disgust at the waves.

It was two whole days before he passed the conch shell again, and heard the voice once more.

Madeline opened the door and nodded in her friendly way. But her voice was weak, and the light glowing from her tail was trembling.

"Hello, Horatio," she sang in D minor, and she glanced anxiously at the house of black coral beside her. A rumbling noise was coming from there, strangely like someone talking at a hundred kilometres an hour.

"Is that your enemy?" asked Horatio.

"Ye-e-es," sang Madeline. "My friend the Kraken usually lives there. We are neighbours now. But the Kraken went to visit his sister who has fallen tragically in love with a merman, and has lost the will to live. How I wish he were here now," and her voice deepened an octave, "instead of that poisonous pest."

"Who is it?" whispered Horatio.

"The Pufferfish!" cried Madeline.

Horatio gasped. He had heard stories about the Pufferfish, the most boring fish in all the sea. The Pufferfish was famous for talking endlessly, using long and difficult words to describe things like the mating habits of the terebellid worm or what his Great Aunt Platter had eaten for breakfast the day before yesterday. As he talked, he puffed up to twice his size with words and importance and deadening ideas. Personally, Horatio wouldn't have minded meeting the Pufferfish. No discussion could last too long for him. Still, others had gone cross-eyed and died of boredom after just two minutes of pufferfish conversation. He was an extremely dangerous creature.

"I'm singing so that I can't hear his dreaded words," sang Madeline.

"And I'm practising my meditation," said

Bella the mercat. "Om, om, om," she purred her mantra loudly.

"But we can't go on being noisy for ever," barked Bella's friend, Byron. "We haven't eaten or slept for days, and still old Pufferfish is droning on."

And in the heartbeat of silence, they all heard him.

". . . and really, Madeline, it is most peculiarly opportune that I discovered the Kraken's residence to be without inhabitants. There will be multifarious opportunities for me to tell you about the manifold branches of my family. I know you are *avid* to hear all about them. My second cousin Tiberius, for instance. Tiberius is *the* great authority on herma— Madeline, where are you?"

At that moment, when everyone began singing and talking loudly again, the current pushed Horatio along, nearer and nearer to the house of the Pufferfish.

"Scream!" sang Madeline.

"Say your two-times table!" wailed Bella.

"What comes after ABC?" barked Byron.

But Horatio kept silent. As the door of the

black coral house opened and a beaked nose shot out, Horatio suddenly knew that his life was about to change for ever.

"Oh, now I see you, Madeline," said the Pufferfish. "As I was saying, cousin Tiberius knows all there is to know about the hermaphroditism of the fairy basslet fish."

"Excuse me," said Horatio. "But what is hermaf— what you said?"

"Hermaphroditism," answered the Pufferfish, "as I was just about to elucidate to our young gelatinous friend, is that condition in which an animal is both male and female – at one and the same time."

Horatio was thinking. On his many travels he had actually met a school of fairy basslet, and he had noticed that they had some very strange habits.

"Pardon me," he said, "but I think what happens is that sometimes the female turns into the male."

"Pardon *me*," exclaimed the Pufferfish, "I am perfectly cognisant of that fact." He turned to Madeline. "I was just about to divulge the fascinating details of this curious phenomenon to you when this mucilaginous person interjected."

"Oh, sorry," Horatio gulped.

The Pufferfish began to breathe heavily, and with every breath he grew larger. In a flash he had doubled his size. Now he looked very dangerous indeed.

Just then the current changed again and Horatio began to drift away.

"Act precipitately," called the Pufferfish, "and inosculate your tentacle around my beak. I wish to continue this line of argument, as one is so seldom acquainted with a jellyfish of such exceptional manners and informed mind."

Horatio wanted to keep chatting too, but he looked warily at Madeline and her friends.

Madeline nodded encouragement, and he saw the glint in her eye.

Without losing another second he shot out a tentacle and latched on to the hard surface of the Puffer's beak. He skidded to a stop. Then he whipped the tentacle around it another ten times.

"Nsosh sho shtightshly!" gasped the Pufferfish.

"What?"

"Undosh shor shtentaclesh!"

"Not until you give us all your promise," cried Madeline.

She grinned joyfully around her, at her beloved Byron and Bella (who had stopped saying "om") and at last at the brave and clever Horatio.

"What golden silence!" she said, and closed her eyes for just a moment. Then she opened them and glared at the Pufferfish. "Promise us, you puffed-up old wind-bag, that you will no longer bore anyone to death."

"Shno!" breathed the Pufferfish.

"Tighten your tentacle, Horatio!" cried Madeline.

Horatio did so, but he said, "Excuse me" under his breath.

"*Now* will you promise, you great garrulous gas-bag? Otherwise Horatio here will keep your beak closed for ever!"

"Shawlrighth, shawlrighth, shi promish!" and suddenly the Pufferfish was free as

Horatio loosened his tentacle and smiled.

"That is the first time I've stayed in one place for more than a wavelength – it was heaven!" Horatio said. "Could I wind a tentacle harmlessly round your tail and hang here for a while? We could talk about your Great Aunt Platter or fairy basslets or whatever you like."

The Pufferfish looked at Madeline.

"You can talk to Horatio," said Madeline, "but if I hear that you have bored him or anyone else, watch out! Because you know what happens when a promise to a mermaid is broken."

The Pufferfish did know, but that's another story. *This* story ends happily ever after, with Horatio having a long, long chinwag (with no interruptions) and a good rest.

And if he stays in one place long enough, even his mamma is sure to drift by.

The Short Cut

Michael Wilson

The really good thing about taking the short cut home from school was that it took much longer than the normal way. Another good thing was that the normal way went past shops and houses and through the town playing fields, but the short cut went along the stop-bank, over a stretch of desert, through a black forest, and past the entrance to the Space Warp.

You didn't go into the Space Warp, ever. Well, Craig didn't. But it was exciting enough just to go past it, and sometimes look down it. Other kids had been right inside, or they reckoned they had, and that's how they knew it was a Space Warp, because you could get to this other planet through it. Lance Harrison

41

said it was not even in the same galaxy as ours, and he'd met these aliens there who gave him messages to take back to our planet, but the messages were a secret and he couldn't tell them to anybody except the Prime Minister. When he could get to Wellington one day, he'd tell the Prime Minister then.

Craig wasn't stupid. He didn't believe everything people told him. But when you walked past the Space Warp, there were these weird noises coming out of it all the time. Like whistling, and howling, and spooky, moaning sounds. Lance said that was how the aliens talked, and he could understand their language now because they'd taught it to him. Once, when they'd both taken the short cut together, Lance translated what they were saying. The aliens wanted Craig to go through the Space Warp on his own, Lance said, so they could study him. He said they were really interested in him because he was so . . . big. (Craig knew he meant "fat". He was just being smart.) Lance said to watch out, because they might capture him and put him in their zoo. Lance had seen their zoo. It was full of creatures from different planets. The aliens weren't interested in Lance because he was too normal.

Then Lance went right through the entrance and into the Space Warp, just to prove that he was safe with the aliens.

Craig felt scared and lonely with Lance gone. He wasn't just not there, he was millions of light years away. When he came back, Craig sniffed and pretended he was laughing. He said he wasn't scared of being put in the zoo, and one day he was going to go through the Space Warp and make friends with the aliens, just like Lance had. Lance said, "OK, why don't you go now? It's their bedtime now, so you'll probably be all right."

Craig's heart started to speed up, and it beat so loudly he was worried Lance might hear it. The funny thing about Craig was, the more frightened he got, the more likely he was to go and do the thing he was scared of.

"OK."

Did he really say that? He had to go now. Actually, Craig suddenly realized he didn't believe any of that Space Warp stuff. He never had, really. It was just a big concrete pipe, and the funny noises were the wind howling down inside it. But he was still scared. More scared than he had been about the aliens. This was real. It was dark, and smelly, and you couldn't see around the corner.

Lance was still going on about aliens. "If you step on an alien snake, you have to suck the poison out in ten seconds, or you die."

Craig just wanted him to shut up now. He was worried about *real* things – darkness, and slime, and not being able to turn around because it was so narrow.

"And if you see an alien, just say, 'Hoo haroo hooweeyoo Lance.' That means, 'I'm a friend of Lance's.'"

Craig started to crawl into the tunnel then, just to get away from him.

"Don't worry, I'll be just here if you need me," Lance said, and then Craig heard him running away through the bush. Craig wanted to keep going, though. He wanted to go on as far as he could, further than Lance ever had, and tell him in front of all the other kids what was really down there.

Craig had to crawl in the pipe. Lance could probably walk along it, although he'd have to scrunch up quite a bit. Turning around wasn't something you'd want to do in a hurry. Craig suddenly remembered stories he'd heard of kids getting drowned in storm-water drains. Was this one of those? What if there was a flash flood? How quickly could he crawl backwards? Craig was scared, but he kept going. He wanted to prove that Lance was just having him on about the aliens. Already he'd crawled quite a way, and if it was a Space Warp, he'd have been sucked right into Hyperspace by now, wouldn't he?

Ouch! What was that? It was slimy, and twisted and . . . a tree root. It had broken right through the pipe and was twisting all round the inside of it, taking up half the space. Well, that settled it – you didn't get tree roots growing inside Space Warps. That was enough proof to take back to school and embarrass Lance with. Craig thought he'd just check out the other side of the root first, in case it was a Sentinel Tree guarding the actual place where the Space Warp really started, and then he'd try and turn round and scurry back out.

There was hardly any room for Craig to squeeze past the root, but at least it was springy and you could push it back. Also, Craig was strong for his age because he was so . . . big.

Which is why he got trapped. The root, which he was pushing back as he scraped his way past, had moved about as far as it was going to. It was starting to slip back. And Craig's tummy had been pulled in about as far as it could manage. When the root snapped back into his stomach, Craig was winded. His tummy muscles gave up the fight, and the root, Craig, and the side of the pipe became one – a jigsaw of tightly locked parts.

Did Craig panic? Well, no he didn't. Not straight away. He knew that when he got his breath back, he could push the root back again and squeeze out.

When Craig heard the voice of an alien coming towards him from further along the pipe – *that's* when he panicked. He knew it was an alien and not the wind, because he thought he could understand some of the words.

"Hoo woo yaroo fat boy. Waroo yeeweeoo zoo hoo!"

They were coming for him!

They were going to capture him and put him in their zoo! Craig tried not to cry. His throat felt all closed up, like a tight fist, but he knew he had to say something. What was that thing he had to say?

"Hooweeoo yoo woo woo Lance!" He shouted it down the pipe. "Weeoo woo haroo yoo Lance! Oo oo weoo yaroo hoo Lance! Lance! I'm a friend of Lance's! Don't capture me, please! I don't want to live in a zoo!"

In the pipe on the other side of the root, Lance was already half bent over, but when he heard Craig's desperate alien pleadings, he doubled right over with laughter. Which was not a good position to be in when Craig struggled free. Somehow, knowing that he had been made to look such an idiot gave him the strength to snap the root right off and bowl Lance over on to the floor of the pipe. All he had to do then was drop on top of him. Sometimes being . . . big wasn't such a bad thing.

"You better not tell anybody about this!" Craig yelled.

"I won't. Promise. It was just a joke. Get off."

Craig still had a lot of yelling to do, so it was a while before he did get off and Lance was able to breathe properly again. It was only after Lance agreed not to tell the kids at school about it, and Craig agreed that it was a pretty neat joke, that Craig stopped to wonder how come Lance had appeared from down the far end of the pipe.

"It comes out by the lagoon," said Lance. "Down the muddy end, by the flax bushes. Come on, I'll show you." Lance took off along the pipe, and Craig found that if he bent right over, he didn't have to crawl; he could actually run, which was a great feeling.

After they'd mucked about by the lagoon for a bit, Craig told Lance how there were these boys in the paper who got trapped in a storm-water drain, and maybe they shouldn't go right into it any more. Lance said OK, and Craig said what they could do was one of them could show kids the Space Warp end, and the other one could be at the lagoon end making weird alien noises into the pipe. They both thought that'd be cool, and started to walk home then, wondering how they would explain their muddy clothes, and how come they were so late.

"Um, we took the short cut?"

Little Obie and the Flood

Martin Waddell

Little Obie lived with his grandad, Obadiah, and his grandma, Effie, in their cabin at Cold Creek, on the Rock River. It was lonely up there, but they liked it.

One day Grandad hitched up the wagon and took Obie down to Bailey's Ford, at the end of Big Valley. They stopped three miles down the track to pick up Wally Stinson, their next door neighbour. He came with them on the wagon.

Bailey's Ford was the biggest place around. There were eight cabins there, and Hannigan's Store. Grandad drove to the store and they picked up the provisions. Little Obie and Wally Stinson helped Grandad load the wagon.

"Looks like bad weather's coming," said Mr Hannigan.

"Yep," said Grandad.

"Rain on the ridge," said Wally Stinson. "I never saw the mountains that black before."

"We'd best be getting back," said Grandad.

That was all he said, but it was enough to make Little Obie think a bit. Grandad never said a lot, that wasn't his way, nor Effie's either, but when he did say something, he meant it. It wasn't just talk.

It began to rain on the way back to Stinson's. Wally Stinson and Little Obie got under the canvas, but Grandad got wet up front driving. The wind and the rain lashed at the canvas, and it was very cold. It was dark when they got to Stinson's cabin.

"Stay awhile," said Mrs Stinson.

"Better get back to Effie," Grandad said. "River'll be rising in the creek."

This time, Little Obie knew Grandad was really worried. He lay in the back of the wagon as it lurched through the rain, and listened to the roar.

The roar was coming from Cold Creek. The

water was rushing and rising. It gurgled round the wagon wheels as they forded the creek, and every minute it rose higher and higher as the rain poured down.

"Never saw the creek so high before, Effie," said Grandad, when they were back in the cabin.

"That's so," said Effie.

"I reckon you should look a few things out just in case we need to be moving," said Grandad.

"Maybe so," said Effie.

"I'm afraid," said Little Obie.

"Now see what you've done with your talk!" Effie said to Grandad. She hugged Obie close. Effie was long and thin, but her body was strong as whipcord. She wanted to give Little Obie some of her strength in case he'd need it, and that was why she hugged him.

Little Obie went to bed, but he didn't get any sleep because of the rain drumming on the roof, the water roaring in the creek and the noise of Grandad and Grandma shifting things below.

"You asleep, Little Obie?" Grandad said.

"No!" said Little Obie, sitting up in bed.

"We'd best be moving," said Grandad.

"Where are we going?" asked Little Obie.

"To the high ground," said Grandad.

They didn't want to be drowned in the rising water, so they had to move fast. They went in the wagon with all the things that would fit piled up on it. Effie drove the wagon and Grandad drove the animals. Little Obie kept in under the canvas, cold and wet and scared out of his skin.

They made it up as far as the high ground beyond the creek, and there they slept, huddled together in the wagon for warmth and comfort.

When Little Obie woke the next morning, there was water everywhere, right down Big Valley. The creek had disappeared, and so had their cabin. It just wasn't there any more.

"Oh!" said Little Obie.

"Don't be afraid, Little Obie," said Grandad. "The water has risen and the river has burst its banks, but the water will go down again."

"Where's our cabin?" said Little Obie.

"Reckon it just washed away!" said Effie.

"What about the Stinsons?" said Little Obie.

"They should be all right," said Grandad. "It's the folks down the bottom of the valley will get the worst of it."

That started Little Obie thinking.

"What about Marty Hansen and her pa?" he said. "And Mr Hedger, and Old Gerd Weber?"

Effie looked at Grandad, and Grandad didn't say a word. He just shook his head very slowly.

"Reckon they'll have got their feet wet," said Effie, but like always it wasn't what she said that Obie listened to, it was how she said it. Her eyes were glistening with tears. But then she wiped her nose, and that dried her up, and she was old stiff-backed Effie again.

"We ought to go and see what happened to them," Little Obie said anxiously. Marty Hansen was his friend and he was worried about her.

"Nobody is going anywhere till the water

goes down," said Grandad. "Specially not down the valley. There's no way we'd get the wagon through."

"Maybe Marty got drowned," said Little Obie.

Grandad and Effie didn't say a thing. There wasn't anything they could say.

It rained all day and the next night too, and then the rain stopped. But the water didn't go away. It kept coming off the mountain and rushing down the valley, and the trees and all went with it.

Then the water started to go down.

It went down all the next day, and the next, and then Grandad said they could try moving down the valley and see how far they could get.

There wasn't anything much left on the low ground but mud and broken trees. They had to lighten the wagon, and even then it sank in deep and they had to move the mud to get it out again, but in the end they made it down to where Bailey's Ford used to be.

Bailey's Ford nearly wasn't there. Most of it had been swept away. But people had come to Bailey's Ford because there was no other place to go.

Old Gerd Weber and the Stinsons and Mr Hedger were there and the Currans and Mr Hannigan, and some of the other folk from the low ground came straggling in, but Marty Hansen and her pa didn't come.

"Where's Marty?" Little Obie asked.

"Nobody has seen the Hansens," Wally Stinson said. "There's no getting down to their part of the valley yet."

"I want to go and find Marty, Grandad," Little Obie said.

"We'll go and look for Marty as soon as we can, Obie," said Grandad. "But there's things that have to be done here first."

They did the things. Little Obie kept thinking about Marty, but he had to be busy too, clearing away the mud and trying to build things up again. There just wasn't any crying time to spare.

"Maybe . . . maybe Marty and her pa went somewhere else?" Little Obie said to Grandad when they were fixing the stall for Curran's hogs.

"Maybe," said Grandad.

"And maybe not," said Effie, hammering away at her stake. It was a cruel thing to say, but Effie didn't mean it that way. She thought Marty was dead, and Little Obie would have to face up to it, and get on with living with the folks who were left.

"Wally Stinson and me will go down the valley in the morning, Little Obie," Grandad said that night.

"I want to go too," said Little Obie.

"You're staying put," said Effie. "It's no business for a child."

Little Obie wasn't staying put.

Little Obie wasn't made that way.

The next morning when Grandad and Wally Stinson went in the wagon, Little Obie went too. Nobody knew he was going because he went in the back of the wagon under the straw.

Effie would have skinned him if she'd known.

There was still a lot of water swirling about the dip in the land down by the rock ridge, where Hansen's place used to be.

There was no cabin.

There was nothing much, just mud and broken trees, trapped against the ridge, where the water had left them.

"That's the end of the Hansens," Grandad said to Wally. "Little Obie will be real upset."

"Old Hansen and that girl, Marty," said Wally Stinson. "Reckon they never knew what hit them."

Little Obie lay there in the straw, with his feelings all huddled up inside, thinking about Marty and her pa in the water.

And then . . .

"Look there!" Little Obie heard Wally Stinson say.

The next minute Wally and Grandad were off the wagon down in the mud, heading for the rocks, and Little Obie was off after them. Only when he jumped off the wagon he fell down in the mud and it was over him, face and all. Then he dragged himself up and tried to run like a little mudball on legs and there was Grandad holding something limp in his arms, dirt-caked and bloody.

"Marty!" Little Obie said.

"Looks like we got here too late," said Wally Stinson.

But Grandad didn't pay any heed. He was holding Marty close and talking to her, trying to make her alive.

Then Marty opened her eyes and looked at Grandad and Obie. She looked as if she could see them, but she didn't show any sign that she knew who they were, or where she was, or what was happening.

She was like that all the way back in the wagon. Wally Stinson made Little Obie stay up front, and Grandad sat in the straw, hugging Marty to keep what life she had left in her after eight days in the wet and cold.

Little Obie wanted to help Marty, but he didn't know what to do, and in the end he just sat tight, close up to Wally at the front. Wally said Marty's pa was dead, and they'd all have to be good to Marty because she would hurt a lot, and maybe they were too late and she would die too, but they'd have to pray that she didn't.

When they got back to Bailey's Ford, Effie and Mrs Stinson took Marty away to Mr

Hannigan's bed by the stove in the room behind the store.

Marty just lay there and people took turns watching her, even Little Obie.

"Grandma?" said Little Obie one day. "Marty's pa's dead."

"Reckon so," said Effie.

"What's going to happen to Marty?" asked Little Obie.

"She'd best come with us," said Effie. "If she gets better."

"I reckon she will," said Little Obie.

And Little Obie was right.

That's how Marty came to Cold Creek, to live with Little Obie.

Effie and Grandad and Marty and Little Obie rebuilt the cabin, only this time they built it up on the high ground, overlooking the creek.

"In case the water comes again," Grandad told Little Obie. "Next time we don't want to get our feet wet!"

Tom and the Dinosaur

Terry Jones

A small boy named Tom once noticed strange noises coming from the old woodshed that stood at the very bottom of his garden. One noise sounded a bit like his Great Aunt Nelly breathing through a megaphone. There was also a sort of scraping, rattling noise, which sounded a bit like someone rubbing several giant tiddlywinks together. There was also a rumbling sort of noise that could have been a very small volcano erupting in a pillarbox. There was also a sort of scratching noise – rather like a mouse the size of a rhinoceros trying not to frighten the cat.

Tom said to himself, "If I didn't know better, I'd say it all sounded exactly as if we had a dinosaur living in our woodshed."

So he climbed onto a crate, and looked through the woodshed window – and do you know what he saw?

"My hat!" exclaimed Tom. "It's a Stegosaurus!"

He was pretty certain about it, and he also knew that although it looked ferocious, that particular dinosaur only ate plants. Nevertheless, just to be on the safe side, he ran to his room, and looked up "Stegosaurus" in one of his books on dinosaurs.

"I knew I was right!" he said, when he found it. Then he read through the bit about it being a vegetarian, and checked the archaeological evidence for that. It seemed pretty convincing.

"I just hope they're right," muttered Tom to himself, as he unlocked the door of the woodshed. "I mean after sixty million years, it would be dead easy to mistake a vegetarian for a flesh-eating monster!"

He opened the door of the woodshed *very* cautiously, and peered in.

The Stegosaurus certainly looked ferocious.

It had great bony plates down its back, and vicious spikes on the end of its tail. On the other hand, it didn't look terribly well. Its head was resting on the floor, and a branch with strange leaves and red berries on it was sticking out of its mouth. The rumbling sound (like the volcano in the pillarbox) was coming from its stomach. Occasionally the Stegosaurus burped and groaned slightly.

"It's got indigestion," said Tom to himself. "Poor thing!" And he stepped right in and patted the Stegosaurus on the head.

This was a mistake.

The Stegosaurus may have been just a plant-eater, but it was also thirty feet long, and as soon as Tom touched it, it reared up on to its hind legs – taking most of the woodshed with it.

If the thing had looked pretty frightening when it was lying with its head on the floor, you can imagine how even more terrifying it was when it towered thirty feet above Tom.

"Don't be frightened!" said Tom to the Stegosaurus. "I won't hurt you."

The Stegosaurus gave a roar . . . well,

actually it wasn't really a roar so much as an extremely loud bleat: "Ba**aa** – ba**aa** – ba**aa**!" it roared, and fell back on all fours. Tom only just managed to jump out of the way in time, as half the woodshed came crashing down with it, and splintered into pieces around the Stegosaurus. At the same time, the ground shook as the huge creature's head slumped back onto the floor.

Once again, Tom tried to pat it on the head. This time, the Stegosaurus remained where it was, but one lizard-like eye stared at Tom rather hard, and its tummy gave another rumble.

"You must have eaten something that disagreed with you," said Tom, and he picked up the branch that had been in the dinosaur's mouth.

"I've never seen berries like that before," said Tom. The Stegosaurus looked at the branch balefully.

"Is this what gave you tummy-ache?" asked Tom.

The Stegosaurus turned away as Tom offered it the branch.

"You don't like it, do you?" said Tom. "I wonder what they taste like?"

As Tom examined the strange red berries, he thought to himself, "No one has tasted these berries for sixty million years . . . Probably no human being has *ever* tasted them."

Somehow the temptation to try one of the berries was overwhelming, but Tom told himself not to be so stupid. If they'd given a huge creature like the Stegosaurus tummy-ache, they could well be deadly to a small animal like Tom. And yet . . . they looked so . . . *tempting* . . .

The Stegosaurus gave a low groan and shifted its head so it could look at Tom.

"Well, I wonder how you'd get on with twentieth-century vegetables?" said Tom, pulling up one of his father's turnips. He proffered it to the dinosaur. But the Stegosaurus turned its head away, and then – quite suddenly and for no apparent reason – it bit Tom's hand.

"Ouch!" exclaimed Tom, and hit the Stegosaurus on the nose with the turnip.

"Ba**aa**!" roared the Stegosaurus, and bit the turnip.

Finding a bit of turnip in its mouth, the Stegosaurus started to chew it. Then suddenly it spat it all out.

"That's the trouble with you dinosaurs," said Tom. "You've got to learn to adapt . . . otherwise . . ."

Tom found himself looking at the strange red berries again.

"You see," Tom began again to the Stegosaurus, "we human beings are ready to change our habits . . . that's why we're so successful . . . we'll try different foods . . . in fact . . . I wonder what fruit from sixty million years ago tastes like? Hey! Stop that!"

The Stegosaurus was butting Tom's arm with its nose.

"You want to try something else?" asked Tom, and he pulled up a parsnip from the vegetable patch. But before he could get back to the Stegosaurus, it had lumbered to its feet and started to munch away at his father's prize rose bushes.

"Hey! Don't do that! My dad'll go crazy!"

shouted Tom. But the Stegosaurus was making short work of the roses. And there was really nothing Tom could do about it.

He hit the Stegosaurus on the leg, but it merely flicked its huge tail, and Tom was lucky to escape as the bony spikes on the end missed him by inches.

"That's a deadly tail you've got there!" exclaimed Tom, and he decided to keep a respectable distance between himself and the monster.

It was at that moment that Tom suddenly

did the craziest thing he'd ever done in his life. He couldn't explain later why he'd done it. He just did. He shouldn't have done, but he did . . . He pulled off one of the strange red berries and popped it into his mouth.

Now this is something you must never ever do – if you don't know what the berries are – because some berries, like Deadly Night-shade, are *really* poisonous.

But Tom pulled off one of the sixty-million-year-old berries, and ate it. It was very bitter, and he was just about to spit it out, when he noticed something wasn't quite right . . .

The garden was turning round. Tom was standing perfectly still, but the garden . . . indeed, as far as he could see, the whole world . . . was turning around and around, slowly at first, and then faster and faster . . . until the whole world was spinning about him like a whirlwind – faster and faster and faster and everything began to blur together. At the same time there was a roaring noise – as if all the sounds in the world had been jumbled up together – louder and faster and louder until there was a shriek! . . . And everything stopped. And Tom could once again see where he was . . . or, rather, where he wasn't . . . for the first thing he realized was that he was no longer standing in his back garden . . . or, if he was, he couldn't see the remains of the woodshed, nor his father's vegetable patch nor his house. Nor could he see the Stegosaurus.

There was a bubbling pool of hot mud where the rose bushes should have been. And in place of the house there was a forest of the tallest trees Tom had ever seen. Over to his right, where the Joneses' laundry line had been hanging, there was a steaming jungle swamp.

But to Tom by far the most interesting thing was the thing he found himself standing in. It was a sort of crater scooped out of the ground, and it was ringed with a dozen or so odd-shaped eggs.

"My hat!" said Tom to himself. "I'm back in Jurassic times! 150 million years ago! And, by the look of it, I'm standing right in a dinosaur's nest!"

At that moment he heard an ear-splitting

screech, and a huge lizard came running out of the forest on its hind legs. It was heading straight for Tom! Well, Tom didn't wait to ask what time of day it was – he just turned and fled. But once he was running, he realized it was hopeless. He had about as much chance of outrunning the lizard creature as he had of teaching it Latin (which, as he didn't even speak it himself, was pretty unlikely).

Tom had run no more than a couple of paces by the time the creature had reached the nest. Tom shut his eyes. The next second he knew he would feel the creature's hooked claws around his neck. But he kept on running . . . and running . . . and nothing happened.

Eventually, Tom turned to see his pursuer had stopped at the nest and was busy with something.

"It's eating the eggs!" exclaimed Tom. "It's an egg-eater . . . an Oviraptor! I should have recognized it!"

But before he had a chance to kick himself, he felt his feet sinking beneath him, and an uncomfortably hot sensation ran up his legs.

Tom looked down to see that he'd run into the bog.

"Help!" shouted Tom. But the Oviraptor obviously knew as little English as it did Latin, and Tom felt his legs sliding deeper into the bubbling mud.

Tom looked up, and saw what looked like flying lizards gliding stiffly overhead. He wished he could grab onto one of those long tails and pull himself up out of the bog, but – even as he thought it – his legs slid in up to the knee. And now he suddenly realized the mud was not just hot – it was *boiling* hot!

His only chance was to grab a nearby fern frond. With his last ounce of strength, Tom lunged for it and managed to grab the end. The fern was tougher and stronger than modern ferns, but it also stung his hand. But he put up with it, and slowly and painfully, inch by inch, he managed to claw his way up the fern frond until he finally managed to pull himself free of the bog.

"This isn't any place for me!" exclaimed Tom, and, at that moment, the sky grew red – as if some distant volcano were erupting.

"Oh dear!" said Tom. "How on earth do I get out of this?"

The moment he said it, however, he took it back, for the most wonderful thing happened. At least, it was wonderful for Tom, because he was particularly interested in these things.

He heard a terrible commotion in the forest. There was a crashing and roaring and twittering and bleating. A whole flock of Pterodactyls flew up out of the trees with hideous screeching. The lizard creature stopped eating the eggs and turned to look.

From out of the middle of the forest came the most terrible roar that Tom had ever heard in his life. The ground shook. The lizard thing screamed, dropped the egg it was devouring and ran off as fast as it could. Then out of the forest came another dinosaur, followed by another and another and another. Big ones, small ones, some running on four legs, some on two. All looking terrified and screeching and howling.

Tom shinned up a nearby tree to keep out of the way.

"Those are Ankylosaurs! Those are

Pterosaurs! Triceratops! Iguanadons! Oh! And look: a Plateosaurus!"

Tom could scarcely believe his luck. "Imagine seeing so many different kinds of dinosaur all at the same time!" he said to himself. "I wonder where they're going?"

But the words were scarcely out of his mouth before he found out.

CRASH! Tom nearly fell out of the tree. CRASH! The ground shook, as suddenly – out of the forest – there emerged the most terrible creature Tom had ever seen or was ever likely to see again.

"Crumbs!" said Tom. "I should have guessed! Tyrannosaurus Rex! My favourite dinosaur!"

The monster stepped out into the clearing. It was bigger than a house, and it strode on two massive legs. Its vicious teeth glowed red in the flaming light from the sky.

The curious thing was that Tom seemed to forget all his fear. He was so overawed by the sight of the greatest of all dinosaurs that he felt everything else was insignificant – including himself.

The next moment, however, all his fear returned with a vengeance, for the Tyrannosaurus Rex stopped as it drew level with the tree in which Tom was hiding. Its great head loomed just above Tom and the tree, and made them both quiver like jelly.

Before Tom knew what was happening, he suddenly saw the Tyrannosaurus reach out its foreclaws and pull the tree over towards itself. The next second, Tom found that the branch to which he was clinging had been ripped off the tree, and he was being hoisted forty feet above the ground in the claws of the Tyrannosaurus Rex!

Tom was too terrified to be frightened. A sort of calm hit him as the creature turned him over and sniffed him – as if uncertain as to whether or not Tom was edible.

"He's going to find out pretty soon!" exclaimed Tom, as he felt himself lifted up towards those terrible jaws. "I bet," thought Tom, "I'm the only boy in my school ever to have been eaten by his own favourite dinosaur!"

He could feel the monster's breath on his

skin. He could see the glittering eye looking at him. He could sense the jaws were just opening to tear him to pieces, when . . . There was a dull thud.

The Tyrannosaurus's head jerked upright, and it twisted round, and Tom felt himself falling through the air.

The branch broke his fall, and as he picked himself up, he saw that something huge had landed on the Tyrannosaurus's back. The Tyrannosaurus had leapt around in surprise and was now tearing and ripping at the thing that had landed on it.

And now, as Tom gathered his wits, he suddenly realized what it was that had apparently fallen out of nowhere onto the flesh-eating monster. I wonder if you can guess what it was? . . . It was Tom's old friend the Stegosaurus – complete with bits of the garden woodshed still stuck in its armour plates, and the branch of red berries sticking out of its mouth.

"It must have given up eating my dad's roses and gone back to the berries!" exclaimed Tom. And, at that very moment, Tom could have kicked himself. "I'm an idiot!" he cried. For he suddenly noticed that the tree he'd climbed was none other than the very same magical tree – with its odd-shaped leaves and bright red berries.

But even as he reached out his hand to pick a berry that would send him back again in time, he found himself hurtling through the air, as the Tyrannosaurus's tail struck him on the back.

"Ba**aa**!" bleated the Stegosaurus, as the Tyrannosaur clawed its side and blood poured onto the ground.

"**Raaaa**!" roared the Tyrannosaur as the Stegosaurus thrashed it with the horny spikes on its tail.

The monsters reared up on their hind legs, and fought with tooth and bone and claw, and they swayed and teetered high above Tom's head, until the Tyrannosaur lunged with its savage jaws, and ripped a huge piece of flesh from the Stegosaurus's side. The Stegosaurus began to topple . . . as if in slow motion . . . directly onto where Tom was crouching.

And Tom would most certainly have been crushed beneath the creature, had he not – at that very instant – found that in his hand he already had a broken spray of the red berries. And as the monster toppled over onto him, he popped a berry into his mouth and bit it.

Once again the world began to spin around him. The clashing dinosaurs, the forest, the bubbling mud swamp, the fiery sky – all whirled around him in a crescendo of noise and then . . . suddenly! . . . There he was back in his own garden. The Joneses' washing was still on the line. There was his house, and there was his father coming down the garden path towards him looking none too pleased.

"Dad!" yelled Tom. "You'll never guess what's just happened!"

Tom's father looked at the wrecked woodshed, and the dug-up vegetable patch and then he looked at his prize roses scattered all over the garden. Then he looked at Tom.

"No, my lad," he said, "I don't suppose I can. But I'll tell you this . . . It had better be a *very* good story!"

NOTE: If you're wondering why the magical tree with the bright red berries has never been heard of again, well the Stegosaurus landed on it and smashed it, and I'm afraid it was the only one of its kind.

Oh! What happened to the Stegosaurus? Well, I'm happy to be able to tell you that it actually won its fight against the Tyrannosaurus Rex. It was, in fact, the only time a Stegosaurus ever beat a Tyrannosaur. This is mainly due to the fact that this particular Tyrannosaur suddenly got a terrible feeling of déjà-vu *and had to run off and find its mummy for reassurance (because it was only a young Tyrannosaurus Rex after all). So the Stegosaurus went on to become the father of six healthy young Stegosauruses or Stegosauri, and Jurassic Tail-Thrashing Champion of what is now Surbiton!*

Titus in Trouble

James Reeves

Titus lived in London in a narrow street beside the River Thames. It was a hundred years ago and more. There were sailing ships on the water right at the end of the street. Titus wanted to go to sea, and the master of one of the ships had promised to take him as cabin boy on his next voyage. But a dreadful thing happened.

One day Titus went into Mr Busby's curiosity shop to have a look round. He often went there in search of telescopes and ships in bottles. Mr Busby did not mind, so long as he broke nothing. But today he was unlucky. Reaching up to take hold of an old ship's compass, he lost his balance and stepped back into a table laden with china and glass.

A pair of tall vases crashed to the ground and broke in pieces.

Mr Busby was furious.

"I'm sorry, sir," said Titus, "I hope they aren't too valuable."

"They aren't *now*," said the shopkeeper. "But before you sent them flying, you clumsy young fool, they were worth every penny of fifteen pounds. I tell you what, though. Seeing you're only a nipper, I'll let you off with ten. Just you run home and bring me the money as soon as you can."

Titus was too dazed to tell Mr Busby that he hadn't a penny in the world. He said he would get the money as soon as he could, and left the shop. Where was a boy like him to get ten pounds? Some boys are good at mending things. Titus only seemed able to break them. There was nothing for it. He would have to go to work to pay for the broken china. Until he had done that, he could not think of going to sea.

"I shall get ten shillings a week," he thought to himself. That was a lot of money in those days. As he strode uphill towards the

City, he sang a song he had learnt from his father:

> *Were you ever off Cape Horn*
> *Where it's always fine and warm?*
> *See the lion and the unicorn*
> *Riding on a donkey!*
> *Hey ho! and away we go,*
> *donkey riding, donkey riding,*
> *Hey ho! and away we go,*
> *Riding on a donkey!*

Presently Titus found himself at the door of a great warehouse. He went boldly up to the manager, and said he wanted work.

"Right-o, sonny," said the manager. "I'll give you seven shillings a week, and you can start straight away."

So Titus got his first job. It wasn't so bad to begin with, but soon the gloomy factory made him sad, and he wished he was down by the river. The smell of the pickles made him feel sick – for that was what the place was, a pickle factory.

Sometimes he carried the jars to the

trolleys, sometimes he stuck the labels on. But whatever he did, by the end of the first week he was wishing he could do something else. Only one thing made him happy – he broke nothing. He dared not.

At twelve o'clock on Saturday, Titus was given his first week's pay, and set off proudly homewards. Then he saw an old woman selling oranges on the quay. The sight of the golden fruit made him thirsty.

"How much?" he asked.

"Tell you what, dearie," answered the old woman. "Mind my basket for ten minutes while I go and get myself a bite to eat, and you can have a couple for nothing."

Titus sat down by the basket, which was perched on the wall at the edge of the quay. Nobody came to buy oranges and Titus looked at the seagulls circling round the masts. Suddenly a great white sail appeared in the distance. Titus jumped up to get a better view, and as he did so he knocked into the basket. The golden oranges rolled over the edge and bounded and tumbled into the river. Titus clutched at the basket and managed to save it, but most of the oranges had gone.

Just then the woman came back.

"What are you doing, you young demon?" she cried. "Just look at my beautiful oranges – all gone to feed the fishes!"

Poor Titus had to give her five shillings of his week's money to buy some more fruit. So she gave him one to eat, and he went home slowly and sadly, with hardly enough heart to suck his orange.

Next Monday Titus decided not to go back to the pickle factory. As he wandered along the street, he came to a printer's shop. Here, a printer was making copies of songs and ballad-sheets, to be sold in the streets for a halfpenny or a penny each. As Titus stopped at the open door, he happened to be singing his favourite song:

> *Hey ho! and away we go,*
> *Donkey riding, donkey riding –*

"So you likes a song, does you?" said the printer. "How'd it be if you was to sing some of these in the streets, and see how many you can sell?"

"I'll try," said Titus.

"Good," said the printer. "Take a bundle of these, and when you sees folks standing about on the corners or in the market, you starts to sing. I'll give you sixpence a day and a penny extra for every dozen you sell."

So Titus set off, and presently stopped in an open place and began singing as best he could. He soon learned two or three ballads, and people stopped to listen to his young, clear voice. The passers-by, especially the ladies, were not slow to buy his sheets. Soon he had sold all his stock, so he went back to the printer for more.

For a whole week Titus went his rounds, singing and selling ballads till his throat ached.

At first the weather was fine, but on the last day of the week a storm blew up; just as Titus was turning a corner, a sudden gust of wind and rain caught his bundle of songs and carried them all away, up the street and over the rooftops. Some went fluttering down into

the street, where they were trampled under foot. Not more than half a dozen could be saved.

The printer took all Titus' wages to pay for the lost ballad-sheets. This made Titus so angry that he went back there no more.

"How shall I ever make ten pounds?" he said to himself. "I can't even make ten pence."

The next job Titus got was in a big store where they sold suits for gentlemen, dresses for ladies and stuff for making coats and frocks. Titus was a messenger-boy. He carried parcels up and down stairs, and ran errands for the manager and the assistants. The manager was an important person called Mr Carmichael. He looked down his nose at Titus and at everybody else. He went about as if he hoped to be made Lord Mayor.

One day Titus was sent from the top of the shop to the ground floor with a huge roll of red satin. Just as he came to the top of the stairs, he tripped. Clasping the end of the stuff with one hand and the banisters with the other, he saved himself from falling; but the roll careered away down the long staircase, just as if it were being laid out for the Queen! The assistants and the customers were almost as surprised as Titus. Then something even more extraordinary happened. Mr Carmichael was at that very moment about to go down the stairs. He was speaking importantly to someone behind him. As he put his foot on the top step, he slipped on the satin and fell. He could not save himself, but went slithering right down to the ground floor. A cry of horror went up from the assistants, who had never before seen their manager in such a dreadful situation. But the customers were delighted, and roared with laughter.

Titus did not wait to hear what Mr Carmichael would say. He took himself out of the building as fast as he could run.

Titus decided to have one more try at earning some money.

"Hey ho! and away we go," he chanted as he strode off towards the big railway station. Surely he could find work there! When he arrived, an express train was about to start for Scotland. Porters were pushing barrows to and fro. Passengers were leaning out of the windows. Friends and relations were pulling out handkerchiefs. Suddenly the guard waved his green flag and blew a piercing blast on his whistle. The engine gave a great roar, and the last door was slammed shut.

Then a man in a check overcoat ran on to the platform carrying two huge bags. He almost knocked Titus off his feet.

"Here, boy," he said. "Take one of these. Quick, follow me!"

Titus seized the bag that was thrust at him, and the man wrenched open the door of a compartment just as the train began to move. He threw the bag he was carrying on to a seat and grabbed one handle of the other. Titus, still holding on tight, was hauled into the carriage. A porter slammed the door.

"I've got to get out!" shouted Titus.

"Too late!" called the porter.

Titus was in the carriage being taken away faster and faster every moment.

"Sorry, boy," said the man in the check coat. "Should have let go, you know. Only thing to do is wait till we get to a station. Then you can take the next train back to London."

On and on they went into the green country-side. Presently the train stopped. They had come to a level-crossing, and the gates were shut. A donkey pulling a cartload of vegetables was in the very middle of the track, and refused to move. So the man at the level-crossing had had to signal the train to halt.

"Now's your chance," said the man in the check coat. "Hop out here. Get back home as best you can. Here's five shillings for you.

Dash my whiskers, what a lark!"

He opened the door and Titus jumped down and made for the road. He had no idea where he was, but he could see the roofs of houses and a church spire in the distance.

Soon he came to a big house at the end of a drive. A huge van was drawn up in front of it, and Titus could see that men were carrying furniture out and stowing it in the van. Two great horses were in the shafts, quietly munching from their nosebags. Titus felt hungry. He went boldly up the steps of the house, and was going to ring the bell when a lady came out carrying a bird-cage with a canary in it. She was crying and dabbing her eyes with a handkerchief.

"Ruined!" she said. "Quite, quite ruined! Yet they must be somewhere! They must, they must."

"Emmeline, Emmeline," said a kind-looking gentleman who had come up behind her, carrying a set of croquet hoops and six mallets, "don't take on so, my dear. We've looked everywhere. There's nothing more to be done. Let us make the best of things."

"Oh Augustus," wailed the lady, "to think it should come to this! If only our aunt had told us where she hid them. But she was always a dark horse, and now she no longer lives to tell us."

Titus couldn't imagine what was going on. He only knew that he was hungry.

"Please," he said, "if you would give me something to eat, perhaps I could find them – whatever they are that this dark horse has hidden."

"My boy," said the gentleman, "I fear you can do nothing, but by all means have something to eat – that is, if there is anything. My sister and I, as you see, are moving house. Our furniture is going to be sold, and we shall have to live in shabby seaside lodgings. We have had to give up this beautiful house, all because our aunt died without telling us what she did with the family jewels."

"I expect she sold them," said Emmeline. "But what is that to you, boy? Come into the house, and I will find you some food. Afterwards, perhaps you'll help us carry our things to this pantechnicon."

Titus was given some bread and cheese, a few grapes and a glass of milk. Then he helped to take things out to the van.

It was a sad sight, all the fine furniture and carpets being packed away to be carted off and sold. Titus began to feel as sad as the poor lady and gentleman.

"Here, my lad," said one of the removal men, "give us a hand with this."

He was holding one end of a chest of drawers. Titus lifted the other end, and followed the man down the steps. He couldn't see where he was going, but managed to reach the bottom without falling. The man climbed on to the tail of the van, still holding the chest. He called to Titus to steady it below, but alas! Titus could hold it no longer. The chest toppled backwards and crashed on to the ground.

"Now you've gone and done it," said the man.

At the sound of the crash, the kind gentleman and his sister ran down the steps. Titus knelt on the ground and tried to raise the fallen chest. It was badly broken. Then he saw something on the stones. Quickly he picked it up. It was a package wrapped in tissue-paper, which had been burst open. Titus lifted out something bright and shining. It was a diamond necklace! Inside the package were more jewels – rubies, pearls, and other precious stones. The crash must have broken open a false bottom in one of the drawers, and the family treasures were at last revealed.

"Oh, what a wonderful thing!" cried the gentleman, pressing the jewels into Emmeline's trembling hands. "What a happy accident! My dear boy, come inside and have some more bread and cheese. Have some champagne! Have anything there is!"

There is little more to tell. Everyone went into the house – Augustus and Emmeline, Titus and the removal men – and as splendid a feast was provided as was possible in the circumstances. Afterwards the men took all the furniture back into the house. The lady and gentleman, their fortunes restored, gave Titus fifteen pounds as a reward for his happy accident.

Titus was so pleased that he hardly knew what to say, but he thanked them warmly, and everyone said goodbye amid laughter and tears of joy. A cab took Titus to the station, where he bought a ticket for London. He was on his way back to where the big ships lay peacefully at anchor in the still water of the River Thames. The handsome reward was safely tucked away in his inside pocket.

"Now I'll be able to pay back the ten pounds I owe for breaking those vases," he said to himself. "After that, it's off to sea I go!"

And sitting back in his corner seat, Titus began to sing joyfully to himself:

Were you ever in Cardiff Bay
  Where the folks all shout Hooray!
Here comes Jack with his three months' pay,
  Riding on a donkey!
Hey ho! and away we go,
  Donkey riding, donkey riding,
Hey ho! and away we go,
  Riding on a donkey!

Yashka and the Witch

Stephen Corrin

On the edge of a forest, beside a lake, lived a poor woodcutter and his wife. They had no children and this made them very sad. The wife was for ever grieving that she had no baby to rock in the cradle, no baby to sing to and care for.

One fine day her husband went into the forest, chopped a nice round log from a tree and brought it home to his wife.

"Rock that," he said.

The wife put the log in the cradle and began to rock it and as she rocked she sang,

Rock-a-bye, rock-a-bye, my little one,
In my little cradle sleeps my darling son.

She went on rocking in this way for one whole day, and the next, and then on the third day, there in the cradle, she was overjoyed to find not a log but a real live baby boy instead. The parents called their son Yashka and as he grew up he longed for the day when he could go out fishing all by himself, in his *own* little boat, on the lake which he loved so dearly.

On his seventh birthday he said to his father, "Dear Father, would you please make me a boat of gold and a paddle of silver, and when I go fishing on our lake I will bring you back as many fish as ever you may need." So his father built him a little boat of gold and a paddle of silver to go with it, and every day Yashka would go out in his little golden boat with his fishing rod, and paddle to the middle of the lake, and there he would fish the whole day long till the sun went down. At midday, though, his mother would bring him his dinner. She would come to the lakeside, cup her hands and call:

Yashka, my son, your work is half done,
Bring me your fish and eat up this dish.

And Yashka would paddle his boat to the lakeside, give his mother the fish he had caught and eat his dinner.

Now the witch, Baba Yaga, the bony one, lived deep in the forest which surrounded the lake. She had heard Yashka's mother call to him, so one day, just before noon, she took a sack and a long hook, made her way to the edge of the lake and called:

Yashka, my son, your work is half done,
Come bring me your fish and eat up this dish.

So Yashka paddled his boat to the shore, thinking it was his mother calling him, and Baba Yaga hooked her long hook to his boat, dragged it to the bank, seized the boy and pushed him into the sack. "That's the end of your fishing!" she gloated, rubbing her skinny hands. She slung the sack over her shoulder and trudged back to her hut, deep in the forest. But as the sack was very heavy and the climb to her hut was very steep she sat down to rest. She soon dozed off, snoring a most witch-like snore. Yashka managed to crawl out of the sack, filled it with heavy stones and rushed through the forest back to the lake.

When Baba Yaga woke up she picked up the sack again and carried it to her hut. Inside was her daughter, more hideous than Baba Yaga herself. "There!" said the old crone, "I've bagged a fine one here," and she tipped up the sack . . . and out came tumbling all those heavy stones. Baba Yaga flew into a most frightful rage. Stamping and shrieking and brandishing her besom, she yelled, "I'll show him. He'll not cheat me a second time." Off she flew in her mortar, beating furiously with her pestle and sweeping her tracks with her besom, back to the lake. In a voice that barely concealed her fury she called:

Yashka, my son, your work is half done,
Come bring me your fish and eat up this dish.

"That's not my mother's voice," cried Yashka. "Her voice is not so thick and rough."

"Not so thick, is it?" muttered the witch. "I'll soon make it finer, my boy, never you fear!" And off she flew to the blacksmith.

"Blacksmith, blacksmith," she croaked. "Forge me a voice, a fine voice, a voice as fine as Yashka's mother's." The terrified smith set to work. "Place your tongue on my anvil," he said, and Baba Yaga stuck out her long, monstrous tongue and the smith flattened it on his anvil. The witch then hurried back to the lake. This time, in a gentle voice, she called:

Yashka, my son, your work is half done,
Come bring me your fish and eat up this dish.

Yashka heard the call and thought it was his mother's. He paddled his boat to the shore. Baba Yaga, hidden in a thicket, quickly sprang out, hooked him in and bundled him into a sack. "You won't get away this time!" she snarled. She dragged poor Yashka in the sack back to her hut and, kicking the door open, she shouted in triumph to her daughter, "Heat up the oven quick, my girl." Then off she swept, while her daughter got everything ready. Yashka hardly dared look at the daughter, so frighteningly ugly was she with her fanged teeth, long hook-like chin and clawing fingernails. He shuddered, but he kept his wits. The witch-girl brought in a flat shovel. "Lie down on that," she shrieked. Yashka lay down on the shovel but he stuck his legs up in the air. "No, not like that!" screamed Baba Yaga's daughter. "I can't get you into the oven with your legs sticking up!" Yashka then dropped his legs over the side of the shovel. "No, that's no good either!" yelled the daughter.

"Well, you show me how," said Yashka.

"This is how!" she snarled and she lay down

on the shovel to show him. Quick as lightning
Yashka pushed the shovel with the witch on it
into the oven and closed it tight. Out he
rushed from the hut and was just in time to
leap on to the branch of a tree and hide
among the leaves, as Baba Yaga came back
into the hut. She called her daughter, but
nobody answered and she realized that the
boy had somehow escaped yet again. The old
crone went black with rage. She rushed
straight out of the hut and made for the tree
where he was hiding. Blind with fury, she
hacked at the tree with her claws and gouged

ADVENTURE STORIES FOR SEVEN YEAR OLDS

it with her fanged teeth. She gnawed and scraped till she broke her teeth. But the tree held firm.

More frantic than ever, she rushed to the blacksmith.

"Forge me an axe to chop down that tree," she screamed. The trembling smith had no choice but to obey, and when the axe was ready Baba Yaga flew back with it to the tree and tried to hew it down. After several mighty blows the tree leaned over, and just as she dealt a final cut the axe struck against a stone so that its blade became chipped and blunt. At that very moment a flock of geese came flying by.

"Geese! Geese!" cried Yashka, "the bony-legged Baba Yaga is trying to catch me. Please, geese, drop me each a feather so that I can make wings and fly back to my mother and father."

Feathers came flying down towards him and Yashka made them into wings. Baba Yaga, in a frenzy, chopped so hard that the tree came crashing down on top of her and struck her dead.

Yashka flew home, and the geese followed. He landed on the thatched roof of his cottage and was just in time to hear his mother saying to his father, "Let us eat to give us strength. Perhaps today we shall find our darling Yashka. Here is some good hot bortsch for you, my dear."

"And what about some for me?" called Yashka down the chimney.

His parents did not know whether to laugh or cry to see him fly into the cottage with his goose-feather wings. They showed their gratitude to the geese by throwing them lots of the choicest grain and seeds.

As for Yashka, after rejoicing with his parents at his safe homecoming, he went, the following day, in search of his little golden boat. And there it was, just where the witch had left it, with its silver paddle, waiting for Yashka to row it away.

Every day he went fishing on his lake, and caught more than enough fish for them all to live happily to the end of their days.

A Picnic with the Aunts

Ursula Moray Williams

There were once six lucky, lucky boys who were invited by their aunts to go on a picnic expedition to an island in the middle of a lake.

The boys' names were Freddie, Adolphus, Edward, Montague, Montmorency and little John Henry. Their aunts were Aunt Bossy, Aunt Millicent, Aunt Celestine, Aunt Miranda, Aunt Adelaide and Auntie Em.

The picnic was to be a great affair, since the lake was ten miles off, and they were to drive there in a wagonette pulled by two grey horses. Once arrived at the lake they were to leave the wagonette and get into a rowing-boat with all the provisions for the picnic, also umbrellas, in case it rained. The aunts were bringing cricket bats, stumps and balls for the boys to play with, and a rope for them to jump over. There was also a box of fireworks to let off at the close of the day when it was getting dark, before they all got into the boat and rowed back to the shore. The wagonette with Davy Driver would leave them at the lake in the morning and come back to fetch them in the evening, at nine o'clock.

The food for the picnic was quite out of this world, for all the aunts were excellent cooks.

There were strawberry tarts, made by Aunt Bossy, and gingerbread covered with almonds baked by Aunt Millicent. Aunt Celestine had prepared a quantity of sausage rolls, while Aunt Miranda's cheese tarts were packed in a tea cosy to keep them warm. Aunt Adelaide had cut so many sandwiches they had to be packed in a suitcase, while Auntie Em had supplied ginger pop, and apples, each one polished like a looking-glass on the back of her best serge skirt.

Besides the provisions the aunts had brought their embroidery and their knitting, a book of fairy tales in case the boys were tired, a bottle of physic in case they were ill, and a cane in case they were naughty. And they had invited the boys' headmaster, Mr Hamm, to join the party, as company for themselves and to prevent their nephews from becoming too unruly.

The wagonette called for the boys at nine o'clock in the morning – all the aunts were wearing their best Sunday hats, and the boys had been forced by their mother into their best sailor suits. When Mr Headmaster Hamm had been picked up the party was complete, only he had brought his fiddle with him and the wagonette was really very overcrowded. At each hill the boys were forced to get out and walk, which they considered very unfair, for their headmaster was so fat he must have weighed far more than the six of them put together, but they arrived at the lake at last.

There was a great unpacking of aunts and provisions, a repetition of orders to Davy Driver, and a scolding of little boys, who were running excitedly towards the water's edge with knitting wool wound about their ankles.

A large rowing-boat was moored to a ring on the shore. When it was loaded with passengers and provisions it looked even more overcrowded than the wagonette had done, but Aunt Bossy seized an oar and Mr Headmaster Hamm another – Auntie Em took a third, while two boys manned each of the remaining three.

Amid much splashing and screaming the boat moved slowly away from the shore and inched its way across the lake to the distant island, the boys crashing their oars together while Auntie Em and Aunt Bossy grew pinker and pinker in the face as they strove to keep up with Mr Headmaster Hamm, who rowed in his shirt sleeves, singing the Volga Boat Song.

It was a hot summer's day. The lake lay like a sheet of glass, apart from the long ragged wake behind the boat. Since they all had their backs to the island they hit it long before they realized they had arrived, and the jolt crushed Aunt Millicent's legs between the strawberry tarts and the ginger-beer bottles.

The strawberry jam oozed on to her shins,

convincing her that she was bleeding to death. She lay back fainting in the arms of Mr Headmaster Hamm, until little John Henry remarked that Aunt Millicent's blood looked just like his favourite jam, whereupon she sat up in a minute, and told him that he was a very disgusting little boy.

Aunt Bossy decided that the boat should be tied up in the shade of some willow trees and the provisions left inside it to keep cool until dinner-time. The boys were very disappointed, for they were all hungry and thought it must be long past dinner-time already.

"You boys can go and play," Aunt Bossy told them. She gave them the cricket stumps, the bat and ball, and the rope to jump over, but they did not want to jump or play cricket. They wanted to rush about the island and explore, to look for birds' nests and to climb trees, to play at cowboys and Indians and to swim in the lake.

But all the aunts began to make aunt-noises at once:

"Don't get too hot!"

"Don't get too cold!"

"Don't get dirty!"

"Don't get wet!"

"Keep your hats on or you'll get sunstroke!"

"Keep your shoes on or you'll cut your feet!"

"Keep out of the water or you'll be drowned!"

"Don't fight!"

"Don't shout!"

"Be good!"

"Be good!"

"Be good!"

"There! You hear what your aunts say," added Mr Headmaster Hamm. "So mind you are good!"

The six aunts and Mr Headmaster Hamm went to sit under the trees to knit and embroider and play the fiddle, leaving the boys standing on the shore, looking gloomily at one another.

"Let's not," said Adolphus.

"But if we aren't," said Edward, "we shan't get any dinner."

"Let's have dinner first," suggested little John Henry.

They sat down on the grass above the willow trees looking down on the boat. It was a long time since breakfast and they could not take their eyes off the boxes of provisions tucked underneath the seats, the bottles of ginger pop restored to order, and Auntie Em's basket of shining, rosy apples.

Voices came winging across the island:

"Why are you boys sitting there doing nothing at all? Why can't you find something nice to do on this lovely island?"

Quite coldly and firmly Freddie stood up and faced his brothers.

"Shall we leave them to it?" he suggested.

"What do you mean?" cried Adolphus, Edward, Montague, Montmorency and little John Henry.

"We'll take a boat and the provisions and row away to the other end of the lake, leaving them behind!" said Freddie calmly.

"Leave them behind on the island!" his brothers echoed faintly.

As the monstrous suggestion sank into

their minds all six boys began to picture the fun they might have if they were free of the aunts and of Mr Headmaster Hamm. As if in a dream they followed Freddie to the boat, stepped inside and cast off the rope. At the very last moment Adolphus flung the suitcase of sandwiches ashore before each boy seized an oar and rowed for their lives away from the island.

By the time the six aunts and Mr Headmaster Hamm had realized what was happening the boat was well out into the lake, and the boys took not the slightest notice of the waving handkerchiefs, the calls, the shouts, the pleadings and even the bribes that followed them across the water.

It was a long, hard pull to the end of the lake but not a boy flagged until the bows of the boat touched shore and the island was a blur in the far distance. Then, rubbing the blistered palms of their hands, they jumped ashore, tying the rope to a rock, and tossing the provisions from one to another in a willing chain.

Then began the most unforgettable

afternoon of their lives. It started with a feast, when each boy stuffed himself with whatever he fancied most. Ginger-beer bottles popped and fizzed, apple cores were tossed far and wide. When they had finished eating they amused themselves by writing impolite little messages to their aunts and to Mr Headmaster Hamm, stuffing them into the empty bottles and sending them off in the direction of the little island.

They wrote such things as:

"Hey diddle diddle
Old Hamm and his fiddle
Sharp at both ends
And flat in the middle!"

"Aunt Miranda has got so thin
She has got nothing to keep her inside in."

"My Aunt Boss rides a hoss.
Which is boss, hoss or Boss?"

Fortunately, since they forgot to replace the stoppers, all the bottles went to the bottom long before they reached their goal.

After this they swam in the lake,

discovering enough mud and weeds to plaster themselves with dirt. Drying themselves on the trousers of their sailor suits they dressed again and rushed up into the hills beyond the lake where they discovered a cave, and spent an enchanting afternoon playing at robbers, and hurling great stones down the steep hillside.

Feeling hungry again the boys ate the rest of the provisions, and then, too impatient to wait for the dark, decided to let off the box of fireworks. Even by daylight these provided a splendid exhibition as Freddie lit one after another. Then a spark fell on Montague's collar, burning a large hole, while Montmorency burnt his hand and hopped about crying loudly. To distract him Freddie lit the largest rocket of all, which they had been keeping for the last.

They all waited breathlessly for it to go off, watching the little red spark creep slowly up the twist of paper until it reached the vital spot. With a tremendous hiss the rocket shot into the air. Montmorency stopped sucking his hand and all the boys cheered.

But the rocket hesitated and faltered in mid-flight. It turned a couple of somersaults in the air and dived straight into the boat, landing in the bows with a crash.

Before it could burn the wood or do any damage Freddie rushed after it. With a prodigious bound he leapt into the boat that had drifted a few yards from the shore.

Unfortunately he landed so heavily that his foot went right through one of the boards, and although he seized the stick of the rocket and hurled it far into the lake, the water came through the hole so quickly that the fire would have been quenched in any case.

There was nothing that any of them could do, for the boat was rotten, and the plank had simply given way. They were forced to stand and watch it sink before their eyes in four feet of water.

The sun was setting now. The surrounding hills threw blue shadows into the lake. A little breeze sprang up ruffling the water. The island seemed infinitely far away.

Soberly, sadly, the six boys began to walk down the shore to the beginning of the lake, not knowing what they would do when they got there. They were exhausted by their long, mad afternoon – some were crying and others limping.

Secretly the younger ones hoped that when they arrived they would find the grown-ups waiting for them, but when they reached the beginning of the lake no grown-ups were there. Not even Davy Driver.

"We will build a fire!" Freddie announced to revive their spirits. "It will keep us warm and show the aunts we are all safe and well."

"They get so anxious about us!" said Montmorency.

So they built an enormous bonfire from all the driftwood and dry branches they could find. This cheered them all very much because they were strictly forbidden to make bonfires at home.

It was dark by now, but they had the fire for light, and suddenly the moon rose, full and stately, flooding the lake with a sheet of silver. The boys laughed and shouted. They flung more branches on to the fire and leapt up and down.

Suddenly Adolphus stopped in mid-air and pointed, horror-struck, towards the water.

Far out on the silver lake, sharply outlined against the moonlight, they saw a sight that froze their blood to the marrow.

It was the aunts' hats, drifting towards the shore.

The same little breeze that rippled the water and fanned their fire was blowing the six hats away from the island, and as they floated closer and closer to the shore the boys realized for the first time what a terrible thing they had done, for kind Aunt Bossy, generous Aunt Millicent, good Aunt Celestine, devoted Aunt Miranda, worthy Aunt Adelaide and dear *dear* Auntie Em, together with their much respected head-master, Mr Hamm, had all been DROWNED!

Freddie, Adolphus, Edward, Montague, Montmorency and little John Henry burst into tears of such genuine repentance and grief that it would have done their aunts good to hear them. They sobbed so bitterly that after a while they had no more tears left to weep, and it was little John Henry who first wiped his eyes on his sleeve and recovered his composure. The next moment his mouth opened wide and his eyes seemed about to burst out of his head.

He pointed a trembling finger towards the lake and all his brothers looked where he was pointing. Then their eyes bulged too and their mouths dropped open as they beheld the most extraordinary sight they had ever dreamed of.

The aunts were swimming home!

For under the hats there were heads, and behind the heads small wakes of foam bore witness to the efforts of the swimmers.

The hats were perfectly distinguishable. First came Aunt Bossy's blue hydrangeas topped by a purple bow, then Aunt Millicent's little lilac bonnet. Close behind Aunt Millicent came Aunt Celestine's boater, smartly ribboned in green plush, followed by Aunt Miranda's black velvet toque, with a bunch of violets. Then some yards farther from the shore a floral platter of pansies and roses that Aunt Adelaide had bought to open a Church Bazaar. And last of all came

Auntie Em in her pink straw pillbox hat, dragging behind her with a rope the picnic suitcase, on which was seated Mr Headmaster Hamm, who could not swim.

Holding the sides of the suitcase very firmly with both hands, he carried between his teeth, as a dog carries a most important bone, the aunts' cane.

Motionless and petrified, with terror and relief boiling together in their veins, Freddie, Adolphus, Edward, Montague, Montmorency and little John Henry stood on the shore – the

fire shining on their filthy suits, dirty faces and sodden shoes, while slowly, steadily, the aunts swam back from the island, and far behind them over the hills appeared at last the lights of Davy Driver's wagonette, coming to fetch them home.

What the Neighbours Did

Philippa Pearce

Mum didn't like the neighbours, although – as we were the end cottage of the row – we only had one, really: Dirty Dick. Beyond him, the Macys.

Dick lived by himself – they said there used to be a wife, but she'd run away years ago; so now he lived as he wanted, which Mum said was like a pig in a pig sty. Once I told Mum that I envied him, and she blew me up for it. Anyway, I'd have liked some of the things he had. He had two cars, although not for driving. He kept rabbits in one, and hens roosted in the other. He sold the eggs, which made part of his living. He made the rest from dealing in old junk (and in the village they said that he'd a stocking full of gold sovereigns which he kept under the mattress of his bed). Mostly he went about on foot, with his handcart for the junk; but he also rode a tricycle. The boys used to jeer at him sometimes, and once I asked him why he didn't ride a bicycle like everyone else. He said he liked a tricycle because you could go as slowly as you wanted, looking at things properly, without ever falling off.

Mrs Macy didn't like Dirty Dick any more than my mum did, but then she disliked everybody anyway. She didn't like Mr Macy. He was retired, and every morning in all weathers Mrs Macy'd turn him out into the garden and lock the door against him and make him stay there until he'd done as much work as she thought right. She'd put his dinner out to him through the scullery window. She couldn't bear anything alive about the place (you couldn't count old Macy himself, Dad used to say). That was one of the reasons why she didn't think much of us, with our dog and cat and Nora's two love-birds in a cage. Dirty Dick's hens and rabbits were even worse, of course.

Then the affair of the yellow dog made the Macys really hate Dirty Dick. It seems that old Mr Macy secretly got himself a dog. He never had any money of his own, because his wife made him hand it over, every week; so Dad reckoned that he must have begged the dog off someone who'd otherwise have had it destroyed.

The dog began as a secret, which sounds just about impossible, with Mrs Macy around. But every day Mr Macy used to take his dinner and eat it in his tool-shed, which opened on the side furthest from the house. That must have been his temptation; but none of us knew he'd fallen into it, until one summer evening we heard a most awful screeching from the Macys' house.

"That's old Ma Macy screaming," said Dad, spreading his bread and butter.

"Oh, dear!" said Mum, jumping up and then sitting down again. "Poor old Mr Macy!" But Mum was afraid of Mrs Macy. "Run upstairs, boy, and see if you can see what's going on."

So I did. I was just in time for the

excitement, for, as I leaned out of the window, the Macys' back door flew open. Mr Macy came out first with his head down and his arms sort of curved above it; and Mrs Macy came out close behind him, aiming at his head with a light broom – but aiming quite hard. She was screeching words, although it was difficult to pick out any of them. But some words came again and again, and I began to follow: Mr Macy had brought hairs with him into the house – short, curly, yellowish hairs, and he'd left those hairs all over the upholstery, and they must have come from a cat or a dog or a hamster or I don't know what, and so on and so on. Whatever the creature was, he'd been keeping it in the tool-shed, and turn it out he was going to, this very minute.

As usual, Mrs Macy was right about what Mr Macy was going to do.

He opened the shed door and out ambled a dog – a big, yellowy-white old dog, looking a bit like a sheep, somehow, and about as quick-witted. As though it didn't notice what a tantrum Mrs Macy was in, it blundered gently towards her, and she lifted her broom high, and Mr Macy covered his eyes; and then Mrs Macy let out a real scream – a plain shriek – and dropped the broom and shot indoors and slammed the door after her.

The dog seemed puzzled, naturally; and so was I. It lumbered around towards Mrs Macy, and then I saw its head properly, and that it had the most extraordinary eyes – like headlamps, somehow. I don't mean as big as headlamps, of course, but with a kind of whitish glare to them. Then I realized that the poor old thing must be blind.

The dog had raised its nose inquiringly towards Mr Macy, and Mr Macy had taken one timid hopeful step towards the dog, when one of the sash-windows of the house went up and Mrs Macy leaned out. She'd recovered from her panic, and she gave Mr Macy his orders. He was to take that disgusting animal and turn it out into the road, where he must have found it in the first place.

I knew that old Macy would be too dead scared to do anything else but what his wife told him.

I went down again to where the others were having tea.

"Well?" said Mum.

I told them, and I told them what Mrs Macy was making Mr Macy do to the blind dog. "And if it's turned out like that on the road, it'll be killed by the first car that comes along."

There was a pause, when even Nora seemed to be thinking; but I could see from their faces what they were thinking.

Dad said at last, "That's bad. But we've four people in this little house, and a dog already, and a cat and two birds. There's no room for anything else."

"But it'll be killed."

"No," said Dad. "Not if you go at once, before any car comes, and take that dog down to the village, to the police station. Tell them it's a stray."

"But what'll they do with it?"

Dad looked as though he wished I hadn't asked that, but he said, "Nothing, I expect. Well, they might hand it over to the Cruelty to Animals people."

"And what'll *they* do with it?"

Dad was rattled. "They do what they think best for animals – I should have thought they'd have taught you that at school. For goodness sake, boy!"

Dad wasn't going to say any more, nor Mum, who'd been listening with her lips pursed up. But everyone knew that the most likely thing was that an old, blind, ownerless dog would be destroyed.

But anything would be better than being run over and killed by a car just as you were sauntering along in the evening sunlight; so I started out of the house after the dog.

There he was, sauntering along, just as I'd imagined him. No sign of Mr Macy, of course: he'd have been called back indoors by his wife.

As I ran to catch up with the dog, I saw Dirty Dick coming home, and nearer the dog than I was. He was pushing his handcart, loaded with the usual bits of wood and other junk. He saw the dog coming and stopped, and waited; the dog came on hesitantly towards him.

"I'm coming for him," I called.

"Ah," said Dirty Dick. "Yours?" He held out his hand towards the dog – the hand that my mother always said she could only bear to take hold of if the owner had to be pulled from certain death in quicksand. Anyway, the dog couldn't see the colour of it, and it positively seemed to like the smell; it came on.

"No," I said. "Macys were keeping it, but Mrs Macy turned it out. I'm going to take it down to the police as a stray. What do you think they'll do with it?"

Dirty Dick never said much; this time he didn't answer. He just bent down to get his arm round the dog and in a second he'd hoisted him up on top of all the stuff in the cart. Then he picked up the handles and started off again.

So the Macys saw the blind dog come back to the row of cottages in state, as you might say, sitting on top of half a broken lavatory seat on the very pinnacle of Dirty Dick's latest load of junk.

Dirty Dick took good care of his animals,

and he took good care of this dog he adopted.
It always looked well-fed and well-brushed.
Sometimes he'd take it out with him, on the
end of a long string; mostly he'd leave it
comfortably at home. When it lay out in the
back garden, old Mr Macy used to look
longingly over the fence. Once or twice I saw
him poke his fingers through, towards what
had once been *his* dog. But that had been for
only a very short, dark time in the shed; and
the old dog never moved towards the fingers.
Then, "Macy!" his terrible old wife would call
from the house, and he'd have to go.

Then suddenly we heard that Dirty Dick had been robbed – old Macy came round specially to tell us. "An old sock stuffed with pound notes, that he kept up the bedroom chimney. Gone. Hasn't he *told* you?"

"No," said Mum, "but we don't have a lot to do with him." She might have added that we didn't have a lot to do with the Macys either – I think this was the first time I'd ever seen one step over our threshold in a neighbourly way.

"You're thick with him sometimes," said old Macy, turning on me. "Hasn't he told *you* all about it?"

"Me?" I said. "No."

"Mind you, the whole thing's not to be wondered at," said the old man. "Front and back doors never locked, and money kept in the house. That's a terrible temptation to anyone with a weakness that way. A temptation that shouldn't have been put."

"I daresay," said Mum. "It's a shame, all the same. His savings."

"Perhaps the police'll be able to get it back for him," I said. "There'll be clues."

The old man jumped – a nervous sort of

jump. "Clues? You think the police will find clues? I never thought of that. No, I did not. But has he gone to the police, anyway, I wonder. That's what I wonder. That's what I'm asking you." He paused, and I realized that he meant me again. "You're thick with him, boy. Has he gone to the police? That's what I want to know . . ."

His mouth seemed to have filled with saliva, so that he had to stop to swallow, and couldn't say more. He was in a state, all right.

At that moment Dad walked in from work and wasn't best pleased to find that visitor instead of his tea waiting; and Mr Macy went.

Dad listened to the story over tea, and across the fence that evening he spoke to Dirty Dick and said he was sorry to hear about the money.

"Who told you?" asked Dirty Dick.

Dad said that old Macy had told us. Dirty Dick just nodded; he didn't seem interested in talking about it any more. Over that weekend no police came to the row, and you might have thought that old Macy had invented the whole thing, except that Dirty Dick had not contradicted him.

On Monday I was rushing off to school when I saw Mr Macy in their front garden, standing just between a big laurel bush and the fence. He looked straight at me and said "Good morning" in a kind of whisper. I don't know which was odder – the whisper, or his wishing me a good morning. I answered in rather a shout, because I was late and hurrying past. His mouth had opened as though he meant to say more, but then it shut, as though he'd changed his mind. That was all, that morning.

The next morning he was in just the same spot again, and hailed me in the same way; and this time I was early, so I stopped.

He was looking shiftily about him, as though someone might be spying on us: but at least his wife couldn't be doing that, because the laurel bush was between him and their front windows. There was a tiny pile of yellow froth at one corner of his mouth, as though he'd been chewing his words over in advance. The sight of the froth made me want not to stay; but then the way he looked at me made me feel that I had to. No, it just made me; I had to.

"Look what's turned up in our back garden," he said, in the same whispering voice. And he held up a sock so dirty – partly with soot – and so smelly that it could only have been Dirty Dick's. It was stuffed full of something – pound notes, in fact. Old Macy's story of the robbery had been true in every detail.

I gaped at him.

"It's all to go back," said Mr Macy. "Back exactly to where it came from." And then, as though I'd suggested the obvious – that he should hand the sock back to Dirty Dick himself with the same explanation just given to me: "No, no. It must go back as though it had never been – never been taken away." He couldn't use the word "stolen". "Mustn't have the police poking round us. Mrs Macy wouldn't like it." His face twitched at his own mention of her; he leaned forward. "You must put it back, boy. Put it back for me and keep your mouth shut. Go on. Yes."

He must have been half out of his mind to think that I should do it, especially as I still didn't twig why. But as I stared at his twitching face I suddenly did understand. I mean, that old Macy had taken the sock, out of spite, and then lost his nerve.

He must have been half out of his mind to think that I would do that for him; and yet I did it. I took the sock and put it inside my jacket and turned back to Dirty Dick's cottage. I walked boldly up to the front door and knocked, and of course there was no answer. I knew he was already out with the cart.

There wasn't a sign of anyone looking, either from our house or the Macys'. (Mr Macy had already disappeared.) I tried the door and it opened, as I knew it would. I stepped inside and closed it behind me.

I'd never been inside before. The house was dirty, I suppose, and smelt a bit, but not really badly. It smelt of Dirty Dick and hens and rabbits – although it was untrue that he kept either hens or rabbits indoors, as Mrs Macy said. It smelt of dog too, of course.

Opening straight off the living room, where I stood, was a twisty, dark little stairway – exactly as in our cottage next door.

I went up.

The first room upstairs was full of junk. A narrow passageway had been kept clear to the second room, which opened off the first one. This was Dirty Dick's bedroom, with the bed unmade, as it probably was for weeks on end.

There was the fireplace too, with a good deal of soot which had recently been brought down from the chimney. You couldn't miss seeing that – Dirty Dick couldn't have missed it, at the time. Yet he'd done nothing about his theft. In fact, I realized now that he'd probably said nothing either. The only person who'd let the cat out of the bag was poor old Macy himself.

I'd been working this out as I looked at the fireplace, standing quite still. Round me the house was silent. The only sound came from outside, where I could see a hen perched on the bumper of the old car in the back garden, clucking for an egg newly laid. But when she stopped, there came another, tiny sound that terrified me: the click of a front gate opening. Feet were clumping up to the front door . . .

I stuffed the sock up the chimney again, any old how, and was out of that bedroom in seconds; but on the threshold of the junk-room I stopped, fixed by the headlamp glare of the blind dog. He must have been there all the time, lying under a three-legged washstand, on a heap of rags. All the time he would have been watching me, if he'd had his eyesight. He didn't move.

Meanwhile the front door had opened and the footsteps had clumped inside, and stopped. There was a long pause, while I stared at the dog, who stared at me; and down below Dirty Dick listened and waited – he must have heard my movement just before.

At last: "Well," he called, "why don't you come down?"

There was nothing else to do but go. Down that dark, twisty stair, knowing that Dirty Dick was waiting for me at the bottom. He was a big man, and strong. He heaved his junk about like nobody's business.

But when I got down, he wasn't by the foot

of the stairs; he was standing by the open door, looking out, with his back to me. He hadn't been surprised to hear someone upstairs in his house, uninvited; but when he turned round from the doorway, I could see that he hadn't expected to see *me*. He'd expected someone else – old Macy, I suppose.

I wanted to explain that I'd only put the sock back – there was soot all over my hands, plain to be seen, of course – and that I'd had nothing to do with taking it in the first place. But he'd drawn his thick brows together as he looked at me, and he jerked his head towards the open door. I was frightened, and I went past him without saying anything. I was late for school now, anyway, and I ran.

I didn't see Dirty Dick again.

Later that morning Mum chose to give him a talking to, over the back fence, about locking his doors against pilferers in future. She says he didn't say he would, he didn't say he wouldn't; and he didn't say anything about anything having been stolen, or returned.

Soon after that, Mum saw him go out with the hand-cart with all his rabbits in a hutch, and he came back later without them. He did the same with his hens. We heard later that he'd given them away in the village; he hadn't even bothered to try to sell them.

Then he went round to Mum, wheeling the tricycle. He said he'd decided not to use it any more, and I could have it. He didn't leave any message for me.

Later still, Mum saw him set off for the third time that day with his hand-cart: not piled very high even, but the old dog was sitting on top. And that was the last anyone saw of him.

He must have taken very little money with him: they found the sooty sock, still nearly full, by the rent-book on the mantelpiece. There was plenty to pay the rent due and to pay for cleaning up the house and the garden for the next tenant. He must have been fed up with being a householder, Dad said – and with having neighbours. He just wanted to turn tramp, and he did.

It was soon after he'd gone that I said to Mum that I envied him, and she blew me up, and went on and on about soap and water and fecklessness. All the same, I did envy him. I didn't even have the fun with his tricycle that he'd had. I never rode it, although I wanted to, because I was afraid that people I knew would laugh at me.

Croc Saw-bones
and Delilah

Farrukh Dhondy

In a nice hot country, once upon a time, of course, there was a broad muddy river with lots of grass and plenty of trees and jungles growing on its banks. In the trees by this river lived a pack of grey monkeys, and in the river there lived a crocodile. The monkeys called the crocodile Croc Saw-bones, because his teeth were like the teeth of a long and wicked saw.

The crocodile swam in the river and sometimes crawled up on the bank and pretended to be a log and slept there in the sunshine. When the pack of monkeys had nothing else to do, they would tease him and

140

throw stones at him.

If old Croc Saw-bones turned round and waddled up the bank to try and catch them, they would run away and, as he came through the grass, they would climb the nearest trees and throw coconuts and other fruit at him. Poor Croc Saw-bones got pelted with ripe fruit which was soft and splishy. The hard fruit just bounced off him.

He tried to stalk the monkeys by plastering his back with mud and digging himself into ditches under the trees. He'd wait for them,

but the monkeys were very cunning. They always saw through his disguises and they knew he couldn't climb trees so they would swing on the branches from tree to tree and get clean away. As they went they would sing a song:

> "See you later,
> Alligator,
> Don't you smile,
> Crocodile
> Silly old Saw-bones
> Dirty old croc
> Thick as a plank
> Smelly as a sock!"

Only one monkey from the pack felt sorry for old Croc Saw-bones. She was a little monkey girl called Delilah.

She didn't believe in being cruel to the old crocodile and she never threw anything at him at all and tried to stop the others from throwing things, but they wouldn't listen to her. It was their best game.

Poor old Croc would wait for all the monkeys to swing away and then he would go down to the river to wash off the splattered berries and guavas and custard apples from his skin. He would sometimes cry hot crocodile tears because he was very angry at not being able to catch the silly, teasing monkeys.

Delilah didn't run away with the others. She would climb the tree and call out to old Croc Saw-bones.

"I'm very sorry that they teased you," she would say. "Did it hurt?"

"Well, not really," the crocodile would say. "I've got very thick skin, you see, but it is a great nuisance. I've already had a proper wash this morning."

Then, after he'd wallowed about and washed, Croc Saw-bones would lie on the bank and Delilah would sit up in the tree and they'd talk.

Delilah liked telling stories. She would remember all the stories her daddy told her the previous night when putting her to bed and she would make up others herself to tell Croc.

All the stories she told were about fairies

and princesses and Father Christmas and goblins and castles and all the old favourites like Cinderella and Snow White, and large and small and wonderful magic people. When she finished a story she would say, "Now, Croc, you tell *me* one."

The old croc didn't know any stories about fairies or magic or castles or faraway places. The only stories he knew were about himself and about what he could see around him. They weren't real stories at all. They were just things that Croc Saw-bones had seen or done.

He would boast about the days when he was young and once he even told Delilah how he ate a whole boatful of sailors.

"I've never seen you eating anything but fish and berries," Delilah said.

Old Croc Saw-bones only sighed.

"I've eaten all sorts of things," he said, remembering all the wonderful meals he'd had. Now that he was old, of course, all he could catch were the fish that swam around him. He didn't know it, but he was a very boastful and boring crocodile.

I'll give you an example. One day, when Delilah asked him for a story, this is the way old Croc began:

"Oh well, yesterday I swam all the way to the other bank. It's quite far but it's easy when you're a big strong crocodile like me and . . . and then I had a little snooze in the mud there. The mud is much cleaner there because there aren't any silly monkeys the other side, you know, so they don't throw paper wrappers and junk on the banks and in the water and then I climbed out and had a little ramble around. There's some lovely fruit just coming into season over there. There are bananas, wonderful huge big bunches of yellow bananas. Oh yes, bananas like there was no tomorrow, little monkey, bananas till the greediest gorilla would fall back with a full stomach and plead for mercy . . ."

That's the sort of story he told.

Delilah had heard that story before because, one way or the other, every story the old crocodile told was the same. He always managed to bring in, in some roundabout way, his trip that day to the opposite shore. And the story was always about the luscious bananas to be had when one got there.

So Delilah would distract him and make him talk about something else. "What's your favourite colour?" she would ask.

"Oh brown," Croc would say. "Oh definitely, no question. Brown. And what's yours?"

Sometimes Delilah would say "pink" or "green", but mostly she liked to make up different shades and colours.

"Lantern blue", she'd say, or "Evening sky orange".

"What's your favourite sport?"

"Oh wallowing," the old croc would say. "No choice there, wallowing every time. A sport for all seasons. The tops, the favourite. Most certainly."

"You know mine? It's gymnastics! I can do cartwheels and double somersaults in the air and swing from branch to branch."

"Mmmm, yes!" Old Croc Saw-bones would say.

"And your favourite food?" Delilah would ask. She had told him twenty times that her favourite food was bananas, but somehow the old croc never answered this question. He would just start munching as though he had bubblegum in his mouth and he would roll his eyes and pretend he hadn't heard the question.

One day, Delilah was asleep in a tamarind tree. She was having a lovely dream in which a handsome prince in fairyland was crossing the ocean on a big sailing ship to the land where a princess was waiting for him. Suddenly she was woken up by a terrible sound.

At first she couldn't make it out. It was a sort of crunching and howling and a low croaking sound. When Delilah opened her eyes she saw it was old Croc crying. "What are you blubbing for, you big baby?" asked Delilah.

"I'm just so sad," said Croc, his tears dripping with big splashes into the river. "I've been for a swim these last two days across the river where I saw these beautiful bunches of bananas just waiting to be eaten. And there was no one there to eat them."

"Well, why didn't you eat them, you wally?" said Delilah.

"Crocodiles don't like bananas, you see," said Croc, "and there aren't any monkeys to eat them on the other shore. It's really sad. Such a waste. They'll just wither on the tree."

Delilah thought for several minutes.

The remnants of the dream of the prince kept coming back to her mind. Then she said, "I'd really like to go and eat them, but I can't swim."

"It's a pity," said Croc. "I'm sure you'd love them. But if you can't swim, well, that's that . . . except . . . er, hang on. I've got an idea. Why don't I give you a piggyback across the river?"

"Because you're not a piggy, stupid, you're a crocodile!" said Delilah. She was joking.

What Delilah knew very well was that her father and the other older monkeys had warned her very sternly against two things. The first one was trying to swim across the river and the second was going too near the old crocodile. Delilah really couldn't swim more than five metres, doing a doggy paddle with her arms, so she knew that the warning against swimming in the river was sensible, but she couldn't understand why they had warned her against the poor harmless old braggart of a crocodile.

In fact, old Croc's suggestion struck her as a good idea. "You mean you can swim with me on your back? And you wouldn't mind taking me across?"

"My pleasure," said Croc. "After all, you tell me the most charming stories which make me think of faraway places and grand halls and rich clothes and magic people. It takes my mind right off this slummy old swamp."

"Well," said Delilah, getting off the tree and climbing on to Croc's back. "I'll tell you the story of a wonderful dream I was having."

"That'll be nice," said Croc, and he turned and swam with his little legs moving in the water and his waist winding and twisting like a smooth piece of rope.

Delilah perched on his back.

She began her story:

"You know, Croc, the story starts where once upon a time there's this very handsome prince. Now, this prince sees an advertisement in the newspaper which makes him very suspicious. What the advertisement in the newspaper says is: WANTED: A HUNDRED WICKED DOGS TO GUARD A DARK TOWER.

"As soon as the prince reads that, he knows that something underhand is afoot. Why would anyone want to set loose a hundred guard dogs in a garden around a tower? Obviously there must be a beautiful princess being kept prisoner in that tower."

That's the way Delilah began to tell her story. When she got to that point she looked at Croc's scaly head. She had never been so close to it before.

"Can't you go a bit faster?" asked Delilah.

You see, she felt something was wrong, because Croc was not swimming as fast as he had been. He was going more and more slowly and she noticed that every now and then he tried to turn his head. But since crocodiles don't have any necks, he couldn't.

"Is something wrong? Are you tired of carrying me on your back?" asked Delilah.

"Oh, no no," said Croc, "I'm fine."

"Then are you bored with my story? Shall

we play favourites? Come on, let's. What's your favourite food? Mine's bananas!"

Croc didn't answer the question.

"Just go on with your story," he said.

You see, what Delilah didn't know was that there *was* an answer to her question. It wouldn't be giving any secrets away to tell you that his favourite food was monkeys. The cruel old fellow liked eating monkeys. In fact, the reason he had brought Delilah out into the middle of the river on his back was because he thought that if he got far away from the shore and the other monkeys, he would dip down into the water, swim under it and turn right round and eat up poor little Delilah.

"All right then," said Delilah. She hadn't even begun to suspect that the old crocodile was thinking evil thoughts. "The prince called his navy and he got sixteen ships and he ordered every ship of the sixteen to be filled full of lovely cottons and silks and wonderfully carved jewellery and every possible lovely-tasting fruit in baskets full of straw and chocolates and skateboards and

dolls and video games and musical toys and anything else that he could think would make a princess happy."

"Then what happened?" asked Croc. This story was getting very good. Then he thought to himself that he'd just try going underwater once, but as soon as he did so his ears filled with water and he couldn't hear a word of the story Delilah was telling. Quickly he came back to the surface.

". . . and so the prince set the pigeon free and it began to fly across the sea towards what must have been land far away," is what Delilah was saying. Oh dear, thought Croc, I've missed a bit of the story.

"Tell me again from where the prince was ordering ships filled with bottles of Coke and cans of dogmeat and all that sort of thing," he said.

"Why don't you pay more attention, Croc? You usually listen so closely to my stories. What's wrong with you today? And anyway, how long will it take you to swim to that shore now and get to those delicious bananas? Hurry up!" Delilah was getting annoyed. This seemed like a long ride. It was even beginning to get dark. This silly old crocodile was playing some very strange games. He kept snapping his vicious jaws.

"The story, give me the rest of the story," croaked the croc.

"Oh yes. Well, the prince had sent the pigeon with a message tied to its feet to the princess."

"Hold on. How did the pigeon know where to go?" asked Croc.

"Because it had come from the princess in

the first place, you fool," said Delilah.

"You didn't tell me that," said Croc. "Is it important in the story? What I want to know is does the prince fight the hundred dogs?"

"I'll tell you that when I come to it," said Delilah.

"That's not fair," said Croc. "Forget the rest of the story, just tell me whether he fights the dogs! I'm getting hungry."

"What's getting hungry got to do with it? We can eat some bananas when we get to the other shore, can't you . . ." she said and her words trailed away because a thought had just struck her. The old crocodile didn't eat bananas. All this dillying and dallying and diving and ducking, what did it all mean? Only one thing was certain, thought Delilah, he was desperate to hear the end of the story.

"Right," she said. "I can't tell you whether he fights the dogs or not, because you wouldn't understand the whole story. That's greedy. It's skipping the main part to get to the end."

"But does he fight them?"

"What do you think?" asked Delilah. She knew now that she had to play for time and they were only six metres away from the other shore.

"Yes, yes, yes, yes, he does, he does. He fights them, he kills them, he wipes them out, the dirty dogs! Yes, yes," said Croc. "And . . . and tell me, what does he do with the dogs after he kills them?"

"I didn't say he kills them," said Delilah.

With a great effort, Croc Saw-bones had turned his head sideways and Delilah could see his big teeth and his big wicked eyeball in the corner of his right eye.

"He does, he does. He kills them and . . . and he eats them!" said Old Croc Saw-bones.

"Nothing of the sort! It's my story, so shut your ugly jaw!" said Delilah.

The croc was just about to say "Oh" when there was a big crash and Delilah felt herself being flung over the Croc's back and onto the soft grass of the other shore. Old Croc Saw-bones had been so busy listening to the story that he'd forgotten to put his headlights on and in the dark he'd crashed into the other bank. He hurt his teeth, but that's not what he was thinking of. He was thinking of catching little Delilah and eating her up.

"Where are you, you little monkey?" shouted Croc.

But Delilah didn't reply. She was desperate to get at the bananas. She ran off and soon found herself in the banana grove that the old Croc had spoken about.

Quickly she climbed a banana tree.

Croc came scampering up.

"Where are you, Delilah?" he called.

"I'm up here, you bad wicked Croc. I know why you were looking at me and ducking and diving under water and getting my fur wet. You want to eat me, don't you? I know why you would never tell me what your favourite food was. Because it was me!"

"Yes, yes, yes, yes, a thousand times yes," said old Croc. "But what I mean is no, no, no, no, no, no, no, no, a million times no. That's not what I want you for. I did want to eat you but now all I want is to hear the end of that story."

"Well, you've behaved very badly, so I'm not going to tell you," said Delilah.

"I'll give you a lift back to your own shore after you've had your fill of bananas, if you'll just finish the story about the prince and the hundred dogs and the princess," said Croc.

"I don't trust you an inch," said Delilah. "But if you want to hear the end of the story, just lend me some money and tomorrow I'll get on the river boat and buy a ticket and get home. Then I'll climb safely into a coconut tree and I'll finish the rest of the story. And if you even yawn at another monkey or open your mouth in front of one, I'll call all the others and we'll pelt you with huge, hard coconuts till you die!"

Poor old Croc. He really did want to hear the end of the story about the prince, the dogs, the princess and the dark tower.

"All right then," said Croc. "I'll go and get my life savings and give them to you to buy a ticket on the river boat. How you expect a crocodile to have any cash I don't know. It just so happens that my grandma gave me a gold tooth once that she'd saved from the mouth of an explorer she'd eaten. I've still got it. I can go and get it, but really, Delilah, there isn't any need. I can carry you back."

Delilah was having none of it.

"No chance," she said from the banana tree, her mouth full of fruit. "Once threatened, twice very shy. So buzz off and fetch the tooth. Remember. No story till I'm safely on the other bank."

So Croc went and fetched the tooth from where he'd buried it. He waited till the morning while Delilah slept up in the tree.

In the morning the river boat hooted at the shore and Delilah swung across from one tree to the next and jumped onto it. The old croc dropped the gold tooth on the deck from the side without being noticed by the boatman and passengers and Delilah paid for her ticket in gold and got a bagful of change. Old Saw-bones swam behind the boat as it crossed the river.

When it reached the other bank, the rest of the grey monkeys were about. They had missed Delilah. She got out of the boat as they watched, and climbed a coconut palm.

"Are you all right?" asked the head of her monkey tribe.

"Just fine. Leave a girl alone," said Delilah.

Saw-bones quietly crept up the mud of the

bank and sat under the coconut palm and snapped his teeth to call Delilah's attention.

"Now tell me the rest of the story," he begged.

"Oh very well," said Delilah and she told him another teeny fragment of the story.

"More, I want more," said Croc. Delilah said he'd have to wait till the next day and she threw him a bunch of coconuts.

"I don't eat coconuts," protested Croc. "No crocodiles do."

"Oh is that so?" asked Delilah. "And no monkeys tell stories."

"OK, you win," said Croc and he ate the coconuts.

The next day Delilah told him a bit more of the story.

"The prince ordered a hundred cans of dog food to be opened."

"And then?"

"Here comes your daily meal of coconuts," said Delilah throwing him another bunch.

Croc ate the lot. He knew if he didn't he'd never know what happened in the story.

Every day Delilah told him a bit more and

made him eat coconuts, peanuts, guavas, mangoes and even bananas. Soon Old Croc Saw-bones began looking forward as much to the coconuts and bananas as to the next instalment of the story.

In fact, fruit became his favourite thing, and by the time they reached the end of that story, old Croc Saw-bones had forgotten all about eating monkeys.

The Voyage of Out-Doing

Susan Akass

Carl and Christopher lived next door to each other. They were friends of a kind. They couldn't do without each other, but they couldn't do much with each other either.

They always had to out-do one another.

When Carl rode his bike, Christopher had to ride his faster. When Christopher shot an arrow, Carl had to shoot one more accurately. When Carl made a den, Christopher had to build a bigger one, and when Christopher collected stamps, Carl had to find ones which were more rare and exciting than Christopher's.

Their houses were near a park. It wasn't much of a park, just a square of tired grass, but it ran down the side of Devil's Hill which

161

was the steepest hill in town. This hill was the scene of some of Carl and Christopher's fiercest contests. When they were small, the boys had run races down the hill. They had run until their legs were a blur, and sometimes they had tripped and rolled over and over to the bottom. When they were older, they had ridden their bikes hell-for-leather down the hill and had burnt out their brakes trying to stop. In later years they had roller-skated, sledged, scooted and skate-boarded down the hill, and they had scars on their knees, bottoms, elbows and foreheads to prove how seriously they took these races.

Now Carl had a new idea. One day, Christopher heard banging coming from Carl's garden, so he looked over the fence. Carl had tools and timber scattered all over his lawn.

"What are you building?" asked Christopher, after watching silently for a few minutes.

"None of your business," replied Carl.

"Are those pram wheels going on it?"

"What if they are?"

"I've got it! It's a go-cart!"

"It might be."

"And so might the thing *I've* been planning for the last few days, except that mine is a four-wheel drive, turbo-charged, injection-fuelled, off-road vehicle, not just a go-cart."

"I don't care what you call it. It won't beat mine!"

"Want a bet?"

"You're on! At the hill, this time next week?"

"Done! This time next week!"

For a week both gardens echoed with the sounds of sawing and hammering, muttering and cursing. The two boys worked in almost total secrecy with only the occasional peep over the fence. They raided their sheds, their lofts and their cellars for wood and wheels, for chains and ropes, for nails and pulleys, for pipes and wires, for nuts and screws and oil and glues. They puzzled and planned and tested and tried, until exactly one week later they whistled their secret whistle across the fence. They were ready for the race.

Carl and Christopher pulled their perfectly designed go-carts to the top of the hill, sat down side by side and wedged their heels firmly into the grass.

"Are we ready? . . . Go!" they shouted.

With a kick and whoop they were off, bumping and clattering down the hill, faster and faster, tearing the turf, scattering dogs, sending seagulls screaming into the sky. There was a dip and a mound halfway down the hill, cause of many a spectacular accident in former races. They hit it at nearly thirty miles an hour and for three seconds both were airborne, before landing again with a bone-rattling crash. Unscathed they raced on, neck and neck, lying low and streamlined with never a thought about how they would stop.

Each hit the fence at the bottom of the park at exactly the same moment, and at exactly the same moment they were both catapulted from their go-carts and flew over the fence to land, simultaneously, in the brambles on the other side.

They did not even argue about it. They

knew, as they picked the prickles out of one another's bottoms, that it was a perfect dead heat. Thoughtfully, they pulled home the crumpled and splintered wrecks that had once been their go-carts.

"Same time next week?" said Carl.

"Same time next week," agreed Christopher.

The boys went back to their drawing boards, this time in total secrecy. Each had to make an improvement to the design of his go-cart that the other could not guess at, for neither could rest easy until he had beaten the other. And so there was a period of silence in the gardens as each thought and thought about winning modifications. Then the banging began again, along with some curious roarings and splutterings and the odd minor explosion.

Race day arrived and the two go-carts were pulled from the secrecy of the two garden sheds where they had been kept under lock and key and twenty-four hours surveillance. They were now somewhat larger and heavier.

They had unrecognizable bits sticking out, some hinged, some on springs, some double-reinforced and some packed under covers. The boys peered curiously at each others' vehicles but made no comments as they heaved them to the top of Devil's Hill.

Preparations for the race took longer this time. Back to back, maintaining their secrecy, the boys fiddled with screwdrivers and tinkered with spanners. Then they checked gauges and meters that had been attached to rather similar new control panels on both go-carts. And this time both boys had helmets to put on and seat belts to fasten.

"I'm ready," said Christopher at last. "Prepare yourself for a shock. You're not going to believe this when you see it."

Carl tightened the chin strap on his bicycle helmet.

"Nothing you've made can out-do what I've engineered," he laughed, sounding supremely confident.

"Right! Are we ready? Let's GO!"

With a kick they were off, bumping, rattling and gaining speed, and again they were neck and neck, burning the grass beneath their wheels. The mound was approaching. Each boy gritted his teeth and, as each hit, there was a roar from his machine, jet engines fired and the go-carts rocketed into the air. In an instant wings sprang out from the bodies of the vehicles, no longer go-carts but jet scooters flashing above the house tops.

Carl and Christopher looked at one another in amazement.

"You spied on me!" screamed Carl. "It was my idea!"

"Never!" bellowed Christopher. "I would never stoop so low. I worked it all out from first principles."

"But the wings! They're almost the same!"

"Inspired by the laws of aerodynamics . . ." shouted Christopher.

"And made from packing cases and sofa springs," replied Carl. "But the jets! What are yours powered by?"

"Solar power, of course. What about yours?"

"Methane gas collected from fermented guinea-pig droppings."

"So yours will run out of fuel! I'll win! Mine will travel on for ever!" shouted Christopher triumphantly.

"Only until the sun goes in!" retorted Carl.

"There's not a cloud in the sky!" laughed Christopher as he increased the thrust of his engine with a touch of a button.

"You can't get away from me!" shouted Carl and he opened the throttle so that his jets screamed with power.

They sped on in close formation, shouting above the roar of the jets as they tried to out-do each other over the brilliance of their machines.

"Mine has sprung wheels for landing," Carl boasted.

"Well, mine has a parachute for a slow descent."

"I've got bags of emergency provisions."

"And I've got a compass for navigation."

They didn't notice anything about their flight. They didn't see the patchwork fields far below them, dotted with tiny sheep and cows, or feel the rush of the wind through their hair. They didn't see the excited groups of people pointing upwards, convinced they were aliens in UFOs. They noticed nothing until the throaty roar of Carl's engine faltered and spluttered. At the same moment, a big black cloud blew across the sun and the pleasant purring of Christopher's engine wound down into silence.

They looked down and then they looked back at one another with horror. They were miles from home. They were flying high over the sea!

"We're going down!" screamed Carl. "We'll plummet like stones into the ocean. It's the end of us!"

"No it's not! Release your parachute," shouted Christopher, pulling his ripcord.

"I haven't got one," wailed Carl. "I'm done for!"

"No! Grab on to my wheel," yelled Christopher. There was no time for Carl to unstrap himself from his seat. He just stretched out and grabbed on. A huge yellow parachute filled with air and slowed the plunging descent of the two go-carts. But they were still going pretty fast. They didn't have time

170

to argue about anything before the ocean was racing up to meet them.

"Brace yourself for impact!" screamed Christopher. Carl let go his grip on Christopher's go-cart, they curled in their seats, hands around their heads and hit the water, splat!

"Now we're going to sink!" wailed Christopher. "Release your seat-belt and swim for your life!"

"Sink? Never!" shouted Carl joyfully. And with a whoosh, four huge air bags inflated around his go-cart. "Climb aboard!" he called to Christopher.

Spluttering and gasping, Christopher swam over and heaved himself out of the water. He flopped into the seat with Carl and watched as his beautiful go-cart slipped slowly beneath the waves, pulling the great yellow bedspread parachute down after it.

"Pity . . . that was a good machine," conceded Carl, "I liked the parachute. Putting that in was good thinking."

"Your air bags are pretty good too. Did your mum know you'd used your camping air-beds?"

"Not exactly. But she said we weren't going camping this year so she won't discover till next year. Did your mum know about the bedspreads?"

"Well, she had said she wanted some new ones."

The boys sat quietly for a while, munching chocolate biscuits from Carl's emergency rations. The little craft bobbed on the waves and the breeze blew them slowly towards land. Then Christopher said, "Who won the race?"

"Why, I did of course! I've still got my go-cart and you haven't!" said Carl with surprise.

"But if it hadn't been for my parachute, you'd have been smashed to smithereens and scattered across the ocean," snapped Christopher.

"True," said Carl, "but you'd be shark food if it hadn't been for my air bags."

"But you'd have been smashed to smithereens *before* I was shark food," argued Christopher.

"Something might have happened to stop

me going down."

"Like what?"

"Like a whale might have caught me on the jet from its blow-hole."

"Fat chance! Where's the whale?"

"Then a whirlwind might have sucked me into the clouds."

"And I might have been carried safely home on a dolphin's back, without your silly air bags!"

The argument continued, becoming more and more ferocious, and neither boy noticed that they were being driven towards a wild coastline of cliffs and jagged rocks. But as he paused for thought, Christopher suddenly saw what was happening.

"Carl, stop talking and look!"

Carl looked hastily around. The cliffs were looming large and the roar of the waves filled their ears. There was nowhere to land.

"There's no hope this time," said Christopher.

"Yes, there is! My rescue flare!"

"Where?"

Quickly Carl pulled a plastic bag from

under the seat. In it was a box of matches and a rocket (lost mysteriously the previous bonfire night). He leant forward and inserted the rocket into a launch tube on the front of the go-cart, then lit the touch paper. There was a fizz and a hiss and the rocket shot up and exploded in a star-burst of colour against the darkening sky.

Would anyone see it? It was their only hope. Furiously, the boys used their hands to paddle away from the rocks, but their efforts were futile against the strength of wind and tide. They were only metres away from the rocks when they spotted the helicopter circling out from the cliffs. As they waved and screamed, it paused, hovering above their heads, and a coastguard was lowered on a rope. He seized them, each under a brawny arm, and they were hoisted skywards. But as they rose into the air Carl began to struggle in the coastguard's grip. "My go-cart!" he yelled in dismay. "Don't leave my go-cart!"

The coastguard couldn't hear much above the racket of the rotor blades, but he was surprised that Carl wasn't more grateful to be

snatched from certain death. He put the boy's reaction down to shock and, in a way, he was right. For Carl *was* shocked, but only about losing his go-cart. Once the boys were safely inside the helicopter he muttered to Christopher, "If I'd got it home I'd have been the real winner, whatever you say."

"But you didn't, did you?" retorted Christopher, as he sipped tea provided by the disgruntled coastguard. "So it's another dead heat."

"I suppose so," sighed Carl.

"Same time next week, then?" said

Christopher, eagerly.

"Same time next week!" agreed Carl, brightening up.

The helicopter swooped back over the cliffs and landed at a remote coastguard station. There, the two boys were hustled into a police car which rushed them home, sirens blaring.

And did Carl and Christopher enjoy all this fuss and excitement? Did they describe the thrills and spills of their epic voyage to the policewoman who accompanied them? No! All through the journey home they sat in silence, eyes screwed up with concentration, planning how to out-do each other in their Mark Three go-carts.

Lost - One Pair of Legs

Joan Aiken

Once there was a vain, proud, careless, thoughtless boy called Cal Finhorn, who was very good at tennis. He won this game, he won that game, he won this match, he won that match, and then he won a tournament, and had a silver cup with his name on it.

Winning this cup made him even prouder – too proud to speak to any of the other players at the tournament. As soon as he could, he took his silver cup and hurried away to the entrance of the sports ground, where the buses stop.

"Just wait till I show them this cup at home," he was thinking. "I'll make Jenny polish it every day."

Jenny was Cal's younger sister. He made her do lots of things for him – wash his cereal bowl, make his bed, clean his shoes, feed his rabbits.

He had not allowed her to come to the tournament, in case he lost.

On the way across the grass towards the bus stop, Cal saw a great velvety fluttering butterfly with purple and white and black circles on its wings.

Cal was a boy who acted before he thought. Maybe sometimes he didn't think at all. He hit the butterfly a smack with his tennis racket, and it fell to the ground, stunned. Cal felt sorry then, perhaps, for what he had done to it, but it was too late, for he heard a tremendous clap of thunder and then he saw the Lady Esclairmonde, the queen of winged things, hovering right in his path.

She looked very frightening indeed – she was all wrapped in a cloak of grey and white feathers, she had the face of a hawk, hands like claws, a crest of flame, and her hair and ribbons and the train of her dress flew out sideways, as if a force twelve gale surrounded her. Cal could hear a fluttering sound, such as a flag or sail makes in a high wind. His own heart was fluttering inside him; he could hear that too, like a lark inside a biscuit tin.

"Why did you hit my butterfly, Cal?" asked the Lady Esclairmonde.

Cal tried to brazen it out. He grinned at the lady. But he glanced nervously round him, wondering if people noticed that she was speaking to him. Perhaps, he thought hopefully, they might think she was congratulating him on his silver cup.

Nobody else seemed to have noticed the lady.

"Ah, shucks, it was only a silly butterfly," said Cal. "Anyway I don't suppose I hurt it."

"Oh," said the lady. "What makes you think that?"

"It hasn't written me a letter of complaint," said Cal, grinning.

As he spoke these words he noticed a very odd feeling under his right hip. And when he looked down, he saw his right leg remove itself from him, and go hopping off across the grass, heel and toe, heel and toe, as if it were dancing a hornpipe. The leg seemed delighted to be off and away on its own. It went dancing over to the bus stop. Just then a number 19 bus swept in to the stop, and the leg hopped up on board and was borne away.

"*Hey!*" bawled Cal in horror. "Come back! Come back! You're my leg! You've no right to go off and leave me in the lurch. And that isn't the right bus!"

Lurch was the right word. With only one leg, Cal was swaying about like a hollyhock in a gale. He was obliged to prop himself up with his tennis racket. He turned angrily to the lady and said, "Did *you* do that? You've no right to take away my leg! It isn't fair!"

"Nothing is fair," said the lady sternly. "What you did to my butterfly was not fair either. You may think yourself lucky I didn't take the other leg as well."

"I think you are a mean old witch!" said Cal.

Instantly he felt a jerk as his left leg undid itself from the hip. Cal bumped down on to the grass, hard, while his left leg went capering away across the grass, free as you please, up on the point of its toe, pirouetting like a ballerina. When it reached the bus stop a number 16 had just pulled up; the left leg hopped nimbly on board and was carried away.

"You're on the wrong bus! Come back!" shouted Cal, but the leg made no answer to that.

Tod Crossfinch, who was in Cal's class at school, came by just then.

"Coo! Cal," he said, "you lost your legs, then?"

"You can blooming well see I have!" said Cal angrily.

"Want me to wheel you to the bus stop in my bike basket?" said Tod.

"No! I want my legs back," said Cal.

"You won't get them back," the Lady Esclairmonde told him, "until a pair of butterflies brings them."

Then she vanished in a flash of lightning and a smell of burnt feathers.

"Who was that?" said Tod. "Was that the new French teacher? You sure you don't want me to wheel you as far as the bus stop, Cal?"

"Oh, all right," said Cal, very annoyed; so Tod packed him in his bike basket and wheeled him to the stop, and then waited and helped him on to a number 2 bus. It was all very upsetting and embarrassing. People on the bus said, "Ooh, look! There's a boy whose legs have gone off and left him. He *must* have treated them badly. Wonder what he did?"

When Cal got to his own stop the conductor had to lift him off the bus, and then he had to walk into the garden on his hands. Luckily he was quite good at that. There he found his sister Jenny feeding her butterflies. She had about forty tame ones who used to come every day when she sprinkled sugar on a tray: small blue ones, large white ones, yellow ones, red-and-black ones, and big beautiful tortoiseshells, peacocks, red admirals, and purple emperors. They were flittering and fluttering all around Jenny, with a sound like falling leaves.

"Ooh, Cal," said Jenny; "*whatever* have you done with your legs?"

"They ran off and left me," said Cal, very annoyed that he had to keep telling people

that his legs didn't want to stay with him.

As Cal spoke, all the butterflies rose up in a cloud of wings and flew away.

"Oh, poor Cal!" said Jenny. "Never mind, I'll wheel you about in my doll's pushchair."

"I'd rather wheel myself about on your skateboard," said Cal.

Jenny was rather disappointed, but she kindly let him have the skateboard.

"Er, Jenny," said Cal, "you don't suppose your butterflies would bring back my legs, do you?"

"Oh, no, Cal," said Jenny. "Why should

they? You haven't done anything for them. In fact they don't like you much, because you always chase them and try to catch them in your handkerchief."

Cal's father said that Cal had better try advertising to get his legs back.

So he put a card in the post office window, and also a notice in the local paper:

LOST
One pair of legs. Reward offered.

Lots and lots of people turned up hoping for the reward, but the legs they brought were never the right ones. There were old, rheumatic legs in wrinkled boots, or skinny girls' legs in knitted legwarmers, or babies' legs or football legs or ballet dancers' legs in pink cotton slippers.

"I never knew before that so many legs ran away from their owners," said Jenny.

This fact ought to have cheered Cal up a bit, but it didn't.

Jenny would have liked to adopt a pair of the ballet legs, but her mother said no, a canary and some rabbits were all the pets they had room for. "Besides, those legs must belong to someone else who wants them back."

Then a friend told Cal's father that one of Cal's legs was performing every night in the local pub, the Ring o' Roses. "Dances around on the bar, very active, it does. Brings in a whole lot o' custom."

Mr Finhorn went along one night to see, and sure enough he recognized Cal's leg, with the scar on the knee where he had fallen down the front steps carrying a bottle of milk. But when the leg saw Mr Finhorn it danced away along the bar, and skipped out of the window, and went hopping off down the road in the dark.

The other leg was heard of up in London; it had got a job at the Hippodrome Theatre, dancing on the stage with a parasol tucked into its garter.

"I don't believe they'll *ever* come back to me now," said Cal hopelessly.

Cal was becoming very sad and quiet, not a bit like what he had been before. He was a good deal nicer to Jenny and even helped his mother with the dishwashing, balancing on a kitchen stool.

"It's not very likely," his mother agreed. "Not now they're used to earning their own living."

"Maybe if you fed my butterflies every day, they'd bring your legs back," suggested Jenny.

So Cal rolled out on his skateboard every day and fed the butterflies with handfuls of sugar. They grew quite accustomed to him, and would perch on his arms and head and hands.

But summer was nearly over; autumn was coming; there were fewer butterflies every day. And still Cal's legs did not come back.

School began again. Every day Cal went to school on the skateboard, rolling himself along with his hands. He couldn't play football, because of having no legs, but he could still swim, so he did that three times a week in the school pool.

One day while he was swimming he saw two butterflies floating in the centre of the pool. They were flapping and struggling a little, but very feebly; it looked as if they were going to drown.

Cal dog-paddled towards them, as far as he could. "Poor things," he thought, "they must feel horrible with their wings all wet and floppy."

They were two of a kind he had never seen before – very large, silvery in colour, with lavender streaks and long trailing points to their wings.

Cal wondered how he could save them.

"For if I take them in my hands," he thought, "I might squash them. And they would have to go under water when I swim. Oh, if only I had my legs! Then I could swim with my legs and hold the butterflies above the water."

But he hadn't got his legs, so he could only swim with his arms.

"I'll have to take the butterflies in my mouth," Cal thought then.

He didn't much care for the idea. In fact it made him shivery down his back – to think of having two live, fluttery butterflies inside his mouth. Still, that seemed the only way to save them. He opened his mouth very wide indeed

– luckily it was a big one anyway – and gently scooped the two butterflies in with his tongue, as they themselves scoop in sugar. He was careful to take in as little water as possible.

Then, with open mouth and head well above water, he swam like mad for the side of the pool.

But, on the way, the butterflies began to fidget and flutter inside his mouth.

"Oh, I can't bear it," thought Cal.

Now the butterflies were beating and battering inside his mouth – he felt as if his head were hollow, and the whole of it were filled with great flapping wings and kicking legs and waving whiskers. They tickled and rustled and scraped and scrabbled and nearly drove him frantic. Still he went on swimming as fast as he was able.

Then it got so bad that he felt as if his whole head were going to be lifted off. But it was not only his head – suddenly Cal, head, arms, and all, found himself lifted right out of the swimming pool and carried through the air by the two butterflies whirring like helicopters inside his mouth.

They carried him away from the school and back to his own garden, full of lavender and nasturtiums and Michaelmas daisies, where Jenny was scattering sugar on a tray.

And there, sitting in a deckchair waiting for him, were his own two legs!

Cal opened his mouth so wide in amazement that the two silvery butterflies shot out, and dropped down on to the tray to refresh themselves with a little sugar. Which they must have needed, after carrying Cal all wet and dripping.

And Cal's legs stood up, stretched themselves a bit, in a carefree way, heel and toe, the way cats do, then came hopping over to hook themselves on to Cal's hips, as calm and friendly as if they had never been away.

Was Cal a different boy after that? He was indeed. For one thing, those legs had learnt such a lot while they were off on their own that he could have made an easy living in any circus, or football team, or dance company – and did, for a while, when he grew up.

Also, he never grew tired of listening to his legs, who used to argue in bed, every night, recalling the days when they had been off in the world by themselves.

". . . That time when I jumped into the tiger's cage . . ."

"Shucks! That wasn't so extra brave. Not like when I tripped up the bank robbers . . ."

"That was nothing."

"You weren't there. You don't know how it happened!"

So they used to argue.

For the rest of his life Cal was very polite to his legs, in case they ever took a fancy to go off on holiday again.

The Creature from the Black Dustbin

Colin Thompson

On Friday nights they always had beefburgers for tea. It had been like that for as long as Peter could remember. Four for his father, three each for his mother and him, and two each for Alice and the dog, Nigel. Then one Friday, quite out of the blue, Peter's mother said:

"We're not eating meat any more," and she put a large pan of strange-looking stew on the table. There were lots of beans drowning in it and lumps of purple vegetables which she said were the healthiest thing in the whole world.

Peter's dad looked depressed but said

nothing. Peter didn't know what to say, and Alice ate three bowlfuls. Nigel sulked under the table. One lick had told him that whatever his mistress had put in his bowl, it certainly wasn't food.

Peter and his dad picked around their plates until Peter's mother went off to the kitchen.

"Here, quick, get rid of all this purple stuff," said Peter's dad.

Peter was about to wrap it up in a piece of paper when his mother came back with a weird-looking cake. He spent the rest of the meal with a very wet pocket.

"Slice of Wholemeal Banana and Turnip cake, anybody?" she said, brightly. Peter's dad went down to the pub where he spent the evening drinking beer and eating pickled eggs. Peter squirmed around in his sticky trousers and Alice ate four slices. Nigel carried his piece of cake out into the garden and dropped it on a fly.

"I'm going to fade away and die," he thought, pushing the cake to one side and eating the fly. Next door's dribbly cat came over the fence, and the miserable dog cheered himself up by chasing it up the apple tree. Later on Alice came out and ate Nigel's piece of cake and forty-eight dog hairs.

Up in his room Peter screwed up his face, put his hand into his pocket and pulled out the purple mess. It felt all warm and slimy like some deep sea creature from the black lagoon. He put it in a plastic box and hid it under the bed behind his comics. He looked at the calendar. It was Friday the thirteenth.

While his mother was scraping the stew off Alice and putting her to bed, Peter slipped down to the corner shop and stocked up on smokey-bacon crisps and chocolate.

Over the next few weeks the plastic box under Peter's bed slowly filled up. The original purple stuff sat in the corner growing a green fur coat and was joined by a whole variety of things as Peter's mother produced more and more amazing meals. There were huge red beans that felt like slugs and little hard white things that looked like tiny eyes. They began to get beefburgers again but now they tasted as if they were knitted out of grass. Even the bread looked grubby.

"Mum," asked Alice, "why's the bread all brown?"

"It's much better for you," said her mother.

"I like clean bread better," said the little girl, and then ate half a loaf with the colour completely hidden under a mountain of strawberry jam.

Nigel the dog was all right. Peter's dad suddenly started taking him for a walk every night and the two of them always came back smelling of vinegar and warm chips. On Wednesdays when Peter's mum went to her yoga classes, Peter's dad brought chips back for Peter and they had to hide the greasy paper in the bottom of the dustbin before she got back.

After a while the food under Peter's bed began to smell. At first Peter pretended it was his socks but when the two ogres who lived in his slippers refused to go to sleep, Peter knew he had to get rid of it. He got down on his knees and reached under the bed for the box. As his fingers touched it he thought he felt it pull away.

"It's probably just my imagination," he said.

He pulled the box out and when his mother went out to the shops he took it down to the dustbin.

"That's funny," he thought, as he carried it downstairs, "it still feels warm."

That night he realized how dumb he'd been. He'd just dropped the box into the dustbin and the next time his mother threw something away, she'd see it. He wasn't too happy creeping round the house at night. Most of the ghosts knew him and most of them were friendly but there were some who only came out on the full moon who were less friendly. And tonight was a full moon.

Peter persuaded the two ogres who lived in his slippers to go with him and he tiptoed downstairs and out into the back yard. It was all pretty quiet except when he went through the kitchen and the lightbulb exploded. The back yard was glowing in the strange blue light of the moon and something felt not quite right.

"Well, we're going back to bed," said the slipper ogres and vanished back into the house.

Peter lifted the dustbin lid and there was the box, but it was open and it was empty. The lid was split from side to side and the inside of the box was perfectly clean.

"Something must have eaten it," thought Peter, but in the dark shadows at the bottom of the garden a pair of purple eyes were watching him. He pushed the container under some rubbish and went back into the house.

After that, things started to go missing from the back garden. Not the sort of things that someone might come in to steal, but odd things. First all the perfume disappeared out of the roses and the earth vanished out of the flowerbeds. One morning all the green mould on the patio had gone.

"It can't be the ghosts," said Peter's mum. "They move things about, but they don't steal things."

"It's not kids," said Peter's dad. "They couldn't take the smell out of the flowers."

"It'll end in tears," said Peter's granny. She was annoyed because she'd left her best boots in the garden and the next morning all the polish had been taken off them. On the same night the air went missing from the bicycle tyres.

Then the howling started. Peter heard it first. He looked out into the garden where the noise was coming from but it was so dark, he couldn't see a thing.

"What is it?" asked Alice, coming into his room and peering out of the window.

"I don't know," said Peter, "but I've a horrible feeling it's something to do with that mouldy food I put in the dustbin."

The howling grew louder but they still couldn't see anything.

"Maybe it's throwing its voice," said Peter.

"Well, I wish it would throw it somewhere else," said Alice, "and stop waking us up."

"Look, there's something there," said Peter, "in the bushes by the shed."

"Purple eyes," said Alice.

As they watched, the eyes moved out into the middle of the lawn. All they could see was a dark shape. The creature seemed to have no arms or legs, no ears or tail. It was just a vague fuzzy shape.

"I think it's a being from another dimension," said Alice.

"What makes you say that?" said Peter.

"I don't know," said Alice. "It looks like it's hovering above the ground. Let's go down and have a look."

"I don't think I want to go near it," said Peter, but Alice was already on her way downstairs. They looked through the kitchen window. The creature was still there, sitting on the lawn eating celery.

"Come on," said Alice, and she opened the back door.

The creature ran off into the bushes but the two children could still see its purple eyes glowing in the dark.

"It's all right," said Alice. "We won't hurt you."

"Promise?" said the creature.

"Who are you?" demanded Peter. "What are you doing here?"

"I am Pesto," said the creature, coming out

into the moonlight. "I am a being from another dimension."

"What are you doing here?" said Alice. "What do you want?"

"I have been sent here from my planet to eat up all the lonely and unwanted vegetables," said Pesto. "We got a message from some carrots that were trapped under your bed."

"Was it you who took the stuff out of the dustbin?" said Peter.

"Yes," said Pesto. "The trouble is that I'm

stuck here. I don't seem to be able to get back to my planet."

"Didn't they tell you how to get back?" said Peter. "Didn't they give you a spaceship?"

"Er, no, they just put me in a big paper bag," said Pesto, "and the next thing I knew I was here."

"Are you sure you're from another dimension?" asked Alice. "Because I keep thinking I've seen you somewhere before."

"You can't have done," said Pesto, "I come from another solar system billions of light years away."

"I don't care," said Alice. "I know I've seen you somewhere before."

In a rage Pesto ran into the bushes and began to howl. He flashed his purple eyes but no one was scared. In fact, Nigel the dog went over and lifted his leg on the creature, and then the howling stopped.

"I know where I've seen you," said Alice. "You're the thing my granny puts her feet on when she's watching television."

Peter went into the bushes and dragged the screaming creature out onto the lawn where

Alice sat on it, carefully avoiding Nigel's wet bit.

"You're just a stupid cushion," said Alice.

"No I'm not. I am Pesto the creature from the black dustbin. I am a being from another dimension. The cushion effect is just a disguise," said the cushion.

"You feel like a cushion to me," said Alice and she dragged it inside to its place by her granny's chair.

"Now you stay there," said Alice, "and if we see you so much as wrinkle your corduroy, we'll pull your stuffing out."

The cushion started to shake. Its corners hunched up like shoulders and tears poured out of its purple eyes.

"I'm *not* a cushion," it insisted. "I am a being from another dimension and I want to go home."

"Well, go on then," said Alice.

"I've told you," said the cushion creature. "I don't know how to."

"We'll help you," said Peter. Now the creature was crying he felt quite sorry for it. "We'll go and ask the ghosts and see if they can think of anything."

Alice was about to say that she didn't believe any of it, that she knew that the thing was her granny's cushion. But then she saw something in the shadows by the couch. It was her granny's cushion. She dragged it out and stuck it down beside Pesto.

"Gladys," said Pesto. "Is that you?"

"Oh, Pesto," said Peter's granny's cushion. "You've come for me, after all these years."

"What?" said Peter.

"Oh no," said Alice. "I don't believe it."

But it was true. Pesto really was a creature from the far side of space and Peter's granny's cushion was his long lost sweetheart who had been sent to Earth twenty years before to rescue some unhappy radishes.

"I've been so lonely," said Gladys. "Twenty years of watching soaps on television every day. I nearly went mad."

"I missed you so much," said Pesto, nuzzling up to the threadbare old cushion. "I'd almost forgotten how beautiful you were."

Pesto forgot all about going home. He and Gladys sat side by side in front of the couch and in the afternoons they watched the soaps together. They had both been lonely for so long but now they were together again. Now they would live happily ever after.

Cherry Pie

Ruth Ainsworth

An old man and his wife lived together in a hut among the mountains. They were poor and hard-working, but contented, and when they sat by the fire at night, the old man smoking his pipe and the old woman knitting, there was nothing in the wide world they wished for – except just one thing which they had given up hope of having, and that was a child of their own.

All the children who lived in the mountain village loved the old couple and on their way to school they would tap on the window of the hut and wave as they went by. On their way home, the old woman would sometimes beckon them in and give them a new, crisp biscuit, shaped like a shamrock leaf, or half a

204

rosy apple. The old man was never too busy to mend the strap of a pair of skates or sew a buckle on a leather school bag.

At Christmas time, the old man and woman liked to give a present to every child in the village, from the babies to the big boys ready to go out into the world. They were so poor that they had to make the presents themselves. They made them of wool which they got from a relation who kept sheep down in the valley. The old woman spun the wool and the old man dyed it bright colours.

Together they made woolly balls for the babies, mufflers and caps for the big children, and dolls for the ones in between. Even the little boys were pleased with a doll dressed like a shepherd or a sailor.

One Christmas, when the presents were all finished, the old woman set to work on something else. It was a big doll, as big as a real child.

"What are you doing?" asked the old man.

"I am making us a little boy," she replied.

His hair was made of dozens of loops of yellow wool and he had blue eyes and red cheeks. She dressed him in a red jersey and navy trousers and soft felt slippers. The old man made him a leather belt and a little wooden stool to sit on. As he sat on his stool by the fire, his legs looked exactly as if he were alive, warming his feet in their neat grey slippers.

"If only he were really alive!" sighed the old woman. "If only he could speak and eat and play about! How happy I should be!"

On Christmas Eve they decided to take their child to the Wishing Well at midnight. The well was named the Well of Saint Nicholas and it was believed that anyone visiting it at midnight on Christmas Eve would have a wish granted. They wrapped the doll in a blanket and carried him to the well. It was a long, cold trudge, the snow sparkling with frost and the stars so large and bright that they seemed no higher than the church spire.

The well was frozen over and the old man broke the ice with a stone before they could dip their fingers in the freezing water and make the sign of the cross.

"Blessed Saint Nicholas, who loves the little ones, grant life to the child we have made."

As they hurried home, their faces numb with cold, the old man thought he felt something stirring inside the blanket. When they were back in the hut, with the door shut, he set the doll down and at once he began capering round the room, dancing and jumping, stopping every now and then to hug and kiss his new father and mother.

The old mother's joy was beyond words. They laughed and cried and kissed each

other while the old woman prepared a bed beside their own. It was nearly morning before the child seemed tired and allowed himself to be put to bed by his new mother. He fell asleep at once, though his parents hardly closed their eyes as they got up so often to make sure he was still there, breathing gently, his yellow head half buried in the pillow.

Now life in the hut was very different. The child was always playing about and getting into mischief. He tangled his mother's knitting and hid his father's tobacco and spilt food on his red jersey. But his parents loved him far too much to be angry.

At first he could not speak, though he soon learned to understand what was said to him; then one day, at dinner, he said plainly, "Cherry pie," which was what he was eating. These were his first words and his parents called him Cherry Pie from that moment.

Cherry Pie loved the other children who came to marvel at him and he soon showed, by signs, that he wanted strong boots and a leather jacket such as they wore, so he could romp outside in the snow. His mother tried to keep him indoors where he was safe, but he pined and refused to eat and spent all day gazing out of the window. His rosy cheeks faded, and fearing that he would become ill, his parents gave him the boots and jacket he wanted, and a cap and gloves too, and he ran out into the snow to play with his friends.

Sliding, sledging, skiing, skating, Cherry Pie could do them all as well, or better, than the others and he soon learned to talk as fast as the others too. He begged to go to school and when he heard the school bell ringing he cried and sobbed till his father made him a school satchel and he went off every morning with his dinner inside, wrapped in a clean cloth.

Now Cherry Pie was a real boy. He could talk as well as everyone else and join in their games and learn his lessons.

"He's a real boy!" sighed his mother happily, as she darned a tear in his jersey.

"He's a real boy, a tough little fellow!" added his father proudly. "He can hold his own even with the bigger ones."

"He's just like us," said the other children when they went home after school. "He's just the same except that he doesn't feel hot or cold as we do, and if he pricks himself, sawdust comes out instead of blood."

But they were all wrong, the father and mother and the children. Cherry Pie was not just like the others. He was different. At first only the priest knew. His mother went to the priest to ask him to christen Cherry Pie and she was bitterly disappointed when he refused.

"Bring him to church – let him read the Bible – let him sing hymns with his friends – but I do not feel I can christen him. I cannot be sure that he knows the difference between right and wrong."

"Indeed he does, Father," said Cherry Pie's mother. "If he has been up to mischief he hides when I come in. He knows he has been disobedient."

"Maybe! Maybe! But I'd like to wait before I receive him into the Holy Church. You're a good woman and you mustn't fret. Go on loving him and bringing him up carefully."

Sometimes the children at school and, indeed, everyone who knew Cherry Pie, were surprised at him. He would kick a kitten out of the way with his foot and when the other children said, "Don't do that. You'll hurt it!" Cherry Pie said, "All right," and he never did it again. Another day he would knock a smaller child over in a game and go on playing as if nothing had happened. When the others called out, "Look what you've done! Her knee is bleeding!" he would pick the child up and never be rough with her again. But that same day he might throw a boy's book into the stove and when his friends cried out, "How can he do his homework? What will he do without his book?" Cherry Pie would give the boy his own book, and would never again repeat that cruel trick.

Once he laughed to see a dead bird in the snow and Franz, his best friend, said to him, "Have a heart, Cherry Pie. Aren't you sad to see it cold and stiff?"

Cherry Pie ran home and asked his mother eagerly, "Have I a heart, Mother?"

"No dear, you haven't," she replied.

"Why not? Why haven't I a heart like everyone else? Tell me why!"

"I suppose I forgot to make one for you."

"Then make one now, this minute!" For the first time Cherry Pie was in a rage and stamped his feet and shouted, "Make one now, before you cook the supper. I must have a heart."

His mother quietly looked out her work basket and some red flannel and made him a heart. He stood in silence, watching every stitch.

"Put it inside me, in the proper place," he ordered, when the heart was finished.

"But it might hurt you. I – I don't think I can do it. Please don't make me, Cherry Pie."

"You must do it," said Cherry Pie sternly. "You must. If you don't I shall run away and never come back. I can't live here without a heart."

So his mother took out her scissors and her needle and thread and her thimble, and she put the heart inside him in its proper place, and sewed him up again. He never moved or spoke till she had finished. Then he jumped for joy and threw his arms round her neck.

"Mother," he said as he hugged her, "what is it I feel beating against me when you hold me close?"

"It is my heart beating."

Cherry Pie put his hand over his own chest and a puzzled look came over his face.

"My heart is still and quiet. It doesn't beat. Why doesn't it beat like yours?"

"I don't know, my little pigeon," said his mother tenderly. "I cannot tell. I would do anything in the world to please you and so would your father, but we cannot make your heart beat."

Cherry Pie grew bigger like the other village children and did more difficult lessons at school and was more useful at home, helping to chop the wood and sweep the snow from the doorstep. Now and then he still hurt someone's feelings without knowing it, though he was sorry when it was explained to him. "I didn't know," he would say. "I never thought – it never occurred to me."

Kittens and puppies and very small children kept out of his way and hid when they saw him coming. He never knew why. He did not wish to harm them. Yet somehow he frightened them and upset them. He knew that he had a heart because he had seen his mother making it, but it did not seem to tell him what to do as it should.

One summer's day, Cherry Pie was walking by himself on the mountainside when he heard a sad bleating. Looking round, he saw a young kid that had somehow become separated from its mother. The little thing ran to him hopefully and began to suck his fingers and the sleeve of his jersey.

"Poor little thing, you're lost and hungry," said Cherry Pie. "I'll take you back to the herd and we'll soon find your mother. She'll feed you and comfort you."

He tried to coax the kid to follow him but the track was rough and stony and he found he had to carry it. Small though it was, it was heavier than he thought possible and he had to stop and rest many times before he reached the grassy alp where the goats were feeding. The kid ran bleating to its mother who was calling loudly for her lost child.

As Cherry Pie went back to the hut for his dinner, he felt a strange, warm glow. He even pushed up his sleeves and loosened the button at his collar. It was a new feeling, new and pleasant.

Another day, Cherry Pie was crouching behind a boulder, watching a chamois and her young one leaping from rock to rock. The mother went first and if the leap was very wide she waited for the young one, turning her head to encourage it and licking it when it was once again beside her. They were so beautiful that Cherry Pie could have watched all day. Their slender legs looked too fragile to bear them as they leaped and frolicked as if they had wings.

Suddenly he noticed that he was not alone. Two hunters were watching also. They held guns in their hands and had hunting knives hung at their belts. He could see the green tassels on their hats and the intent look on their faces.

Cherry Pie only knew the chamois were in danger and he ran forward, waving his arms and shouting. In a second the two animals

were out of sight. He did not wait to hear the angry words of the huntsmen. He hurried home feeling, for the second time, a lovely glow of warmth.

"How rosy your cheeks are!" said his mother when he got back to the hut.

Some days later Cherry Pie was out for a walk with his friend Franz. Cherry Pie was wearing a pair of new boots his father had made. They had clusters of nails on the soles so he would not slip and the laces were tough leather thongs. The nails made patterns where the snow was soft. He felt proud as he strode along, proud of his stout, strong boots such as big boys wore.

The two boys climbed higher and higher above the village and nearer to the great glacier, the Sea of Glass, which was famous for many miles around.

"Shall we turn back?" said Franz. "I've never been as high as this without my father."

"Nor have I," said Cherry Pie, "but let's go on a little way. Let's go to the edge of the Sea of Glass and just set foot on it. Then we'll turn back."

"We haven't a rope," said Franz, "or an ice axe. Perhaps we should turn back now."

"Oh, we're all right," said Cherry Pie. "My new boots won't slip. They can't slip, they're so well nailed."

"My boots aren't new," muttered Franz. "They're old and the nails are worn down."

"I'll hold your hand and then you'll feel safe," said Cherry Pie.

The Sea of Glass was so beautiful that the boys were glad they had come so far. It was blue and shone so brightly that they had to screw up their eyes. They tried a few steps on its polished surface, Cherry Pie going first, but almost at once Franz gave a cry of terror and there was a crackling, slithering sound. He had fallen down a crevasse, a deep crack in the ice.

Cherry Pie lay flat and peered over the edge. It was dark and horrible, but he could see Franz's blue cap far below.

"Are you all right, Franz?"

"Yes. I'm caught on a ledge but it's very narrow."

"Hold on. I'll let down my scarf and pull you up."

Cherry Pie unwound the long warm scarf his mother had knitted and lowered it down the crack.

"Can you reach the end, Franz?"

"No," came Franz's voice. "No. It isn't long enough."

Cherry Pie undid the leather belt his father had made and fixed it on to the scarf. He lowered this down the crevasse.

"Hold on, Franz."

The answer came more faintly. "I can't quite reach."

Cherry Pie thought quickly. What could he add to his home-made rope? A sock, perhaps? His jersey? Then he remembered his leather bootlaces. Fumbling in his hurry he undid one lace, then the other, and knotted them on to the end. This time Franz's voice said, "Yes. I've got it. I'm holding on."

"I'm going to pull you up," said Cherry Pie, but he found that he was not strong enough. He could not raise Franz an inch.

"You must hold on to your end and I'll hold on to mine," said Cherry Pie. "Someone will pass by and they will help. Just hold on."

Both boys held on, knowing that few people passed that way, especially in winter. It was a lucky chance that the priest went by, as dusk was gathering, having visited a sick woman in the next village. He was able to rescue Franz and carry him home, Cherry Pie stumbling along beside him. Stiff and numb though he was, he felt the strange warmth spreading even to his icy hands and feet.

When he lay in front of the fire, wrapped in blankets, his father and mother rubbing him and petting him, he suddenly cried out, "My heart is beating! My heart is beating at last! Father! Mother! Feel it beating! That's why I felt warm even when I was lying on the ice."

Now the family in the hut had nothing else to wish for. They did not need to visit St Nicholas's Well again. The priest gladly christened Cherry Pie and from that time he never hurt anyone's feelings and the little children and animals ran to meet him, instead of hiding. His red flannel heart worked as well as everyone else's and told him what to do.

Saki, the Boy Hunter

Lorle Harris

Famine threatened the village that was the home of Saki, the boy hunter. Every day the men went out in search of food. Some climbed into their canoes armed with spears, nets and fish hooks. Others slung quivers filled with arrows over their shoulders, and clasping their bows firmly in their hands, trudged into the woods. Every day they came home with a few little fish and a skinny rabbit or two – only a mouthful for each villager after the food was divided.

Saki, too, went out every day. Although he was known for his skill with the bow and arrow, his luck wasn't any better than the men's.

One day when Saki hunted, he came upon a

221

little animal that looked like a dog, but he was so bedraggled and dirty, Saki couldn't be sure. He took the dog home and washed him. He shared his meal of porcupine meat with his new friend, giving him the larger portion. Then to be sure he wouldn't mistake the dog for his prey when hunting, he dabbed red paint on the animal's head and feet.

The very next day, Saki and the dog went into the forest. The dog flushed out grouse from their hiding places and brought them to Saki. He tracked down a mountain sheep. Saki was so pleased with his hunting companion, he gave him the best part of the meat. The remainder Saki shared with his family and friends.

When Saki's brother-in-law saw what a fine hunting dog Saki had, he asked to borrow the animal. Saki put red paint on the dog's feet and around his mouth. "You may take him," Saki said, "but be sure to give him the first sheep you kill. That is what I always do."

When the man returned from the hunt, the dog was not with him.

"Where is my little dog?" Saki asked.

"He ran away."

That's strange, thought Saki, he must have had a reason for running away.

Saki went to his sister. "What did your husband do with my dog?" he asked. "Tell me the truth."

"He threw entrails to the dog," she said. "The dog refused to eat them and ran straight up between the mountains."

"I was afraid that would happen."

Saki went to his brother-in-law. "Show me where the dog disappeared."

His brother-in-law took Saki to the spot where the dog fled into the mountains. Scrutinizing every inch of ground for footprints smudged with red paint, Saki plodded along. At last he found them.

The footprints led to a large lake. Saki saw a town on the far side, but how was he to get across? He paced back and forth. If only I had a canoe, he thought.

After a while the smell of smoke tickled his nose. His eyes watered. Was that a column of smoke curling up from beneath his feet? Saki stepped to one side.

A door in the earth opened and a woman's voice said, "Come in."

Saki felt his way down the log ladder with its wedge-shaped footholds. The flickering flames from the hearth cast eerie shadows on the cave-like walls of the underground house. Saki strained his eyes to make out the stooped figure of a tiny woman.

"What brought you here, Grandchild?" she asked.

Saki told her of the dog he befriended, and how the dog had helped him, but was now lost.

"Your dog must be the Wolf Chief's Son," the old woman said, "he lives on the other side of the lake."

"But how . . ."

The old woman read his mind. "Take my little canoe. Don't worry, it won't turn over with you. When you have carried it to the shore, shake it and it will become large enough for you. But don't paddle the boat," she continued, "lie down in the bottom. Concentrate on where you want to go and the canoe will take you there."

Saki did as he was told and landed safely on the other side of the lake. When he stepped out of the boat, he wished the canoe small. He watched the canoe shrink smaller and smaller. It shrank so much, Saki folded it and put it away.

Saki walked along the beach until he met some boys playing with a deeply arched bow. Its colours flashed blue, red, yellow and green as they tossed the bow about.

"Where does the Wolf Chief live?" Saki asked.

The boys pointed to a house at the far end of the village.

Saki slipped into the house. He crept behind the wolf people gathered around the hearth – and there, lying in front of his father, was Saki's friend.

"I feel the eyes of a human being upon us," the Wolf Chief said. "Where is he hiding?"

The little wolf put his nose to the ground and followed the man-scent to Saki. Little wolf was so happy to see his friend, he jumped up on him and licked his face.

Then the father knew who the boy was. "I

am pleased that you cared enough to search for my son. I sent him to live among your people because I knew you were starving and he could help you. We are happy to have you as our guest."

Little Wolf and Saki played by the fire. The wolf people brought Saki bear and mountain sheep meat to eat.

When the time came for Saki to go home, the Wolf Chief said, "Some of your people didn't treat my son properly. He will not return to the village with you, but I will give you some charms instead."

He had hardly finished speaking when Saki saw the Wolf Chief had taken the form of a human being. The man pointed to a fish-hawk's quill hanging on the wall. "Bring it to me," he ordered his son.

The Wolf Chief took the quill in his hand. Squinting his eyes, he aimed the quill at the opening above the hearth. The quill flew through the smoke hole. Wolf Chief motioned to Little Wolf to get the quill.

"Whenever you meet a bear, Saki, point the quill directly at him," Wolf Chief said, "and it will pierce his heart." He handed Saki the quill.

Then Wolf Chief showed Saki a large robe, neatly folded and tied like a blanket. "This is the mantle of life and death," he said gravely. He unfolded the robe. "This side cures illness. Place the soft warm fur next to the sick person's skin – so."

He shook the mantle so it billowed like a blanket buffeted by the wind, then settled gently on the ground. He turned the mantle over. "The hide side is rough and cold. It will bring death." Handing Saki the mantle, he said, "Use it wisely."

Saki turned to leave.

"Do you see that great curved bow the boys are playing with?" Wolf Chief asked. "That's my rainbow. When you see it in the evening sky, it warns of bad weather. Take shelter 'till the sun comes out. If you see it in the morning, it will be a fine day."

Then the chief put a pebble-like object in Saki's mouth. It tasted sweet as blackberries and succulent as the tenderest of meats. "Take this," the Wolf Chief said. "Although the days of your journey will be many, they will seem but a few."

And so it was. When Saki came to the cleft in the mountains where Wolf Chief's son had disappeared, he knew he was almost home. He hurried along the path that led to his village.

Suddenly a huge grizzly bear stepped out of the woods, rearing up in front of Saki! Saki drew the magic quill from his pocket, and aimed it straight at the bear. Just as Wolf Chief had said, the quill flew directly towards the bear's heart!

Shortly afterward, Saki came upon a flock of mountain sheep. The sheep were grazing so close together it was impossible to single out one animal. Saki aimed his quill at the flock. One by one the sheep toppled over!

Saki examined his prey. The quill struck every one of the sheep, he thought wonderingly. He cut up the meat. When he came to the last sheep, he found the quill embedded in its heart.

Saki ate a little, then dug a cache in the ground. My people will have enough meat to last a long time, he thought. He covered and marked the cache so he could find it again.

Now Saki could hardly wait to get home. He ran so fast his feet barely touched the ground.

The village was strangely quiet when he reached the row of houses facing the sea. No children played on the beach. No murmur of women's voices, chatting as they went about their work, reached his ears. Where was everyone?

Saki ran towards his house. His little cousin lay in front of the doorway. Saki bent over her. She looks like a bundle of bones, he thought, placing his ear against her chest. There was no heartbeat!

Saki quickly unwrapped the mantle the wolf chief had given him. He threw it over the little girl, making sure the life-giving side touched her body.

The child stirred. She stretched out her arms as if awakening from a night's sleep. "Saki, Saki," she said, "where have you been?"

"Visiting the wolf people. Where's everybody?"

"They're all asleep."

Saki crept inside the house. Silence enveloped him like a thick blanket of fog. He climbed on the sleeping platform where his aunt and uncle lay. Both were dead. Saki threw the magic mantle over his uncle, and then over his aunt. They sat up!

"I've plenty of food for everyone," Saki said proudly. "I'll wake up everyone and we'll go after it." He pushed aside the blankets that separated his family's sleeping quarters from the next. He visited each section of the sleeping platform in turn, waking each person with his wonderful robe.

Then Saki led his people to the place where he had stored the meat of the mountain sheep. What a feast they had! What they couldn't finish, they carried home.

After that, whenever the people needed meat, Saki hunted with his magic fish-hawk's quill. When his people fell ill, he cured them with his magic blanket. And the people paid him for his services, so that he became a very rich man.

Blankets and furs, finely carved feast bowls, and painted storage boxes piled up in his house. When he had enough gifts for the chiefs in the neighbouring villages, he held a great potlatch and gave away all he had.

Again and again Saki invited his neighbours to a giveaway feast. After each potlatch his wife took his cedar root hat and added a new strip to the topknot to commemorate the event. From the height of his hat everyone knew Saki was a great and powerful man.

ACKNOWLEDGEMENTS

The publishers wish to thank the following for permission to reproduce copyright material:

Joan Aiken: for "Lost – One Pair of Legs" from *The Last Slice of the Rainbow* by Joan Aiken, 1985. Copyright © Joan Aiken Enterprises Ltd, by permission of A M Heath & Co Ltd on behalf of the author.

Ruth Ainsworth: for "Cherry Pie", by permission of R F Gilbert.

Susan Akass: for "The Voyage of Out-doing" from *Story of the Year 1993*, Scholastic, 1993, pp. 79–93, by permission of Scholastic Ltd.

Stephen Corrin: for "Yashka and the Witch" from *More Stories for Seven Year Olds and Other Young Readers* eds. Sarah and Stephen Corrin, Faber & Faber Ltd, 1978, pp. 62–66, by permission of Faber & Faber Ltd.

Farrukh Dhondy: for "Croc Saw-bones and Delilah" from *Janaky and the Giant and Other Stories* by Farrukh Dhondy, HarperCollins, 1993, pp. 66–82, by permission of David Higham Associates on behalf of the author.

Anna Fienberg: for "Horatio the Jellyfish" from *Madeline the Mermaid and Other Fishy Tales* by Anna Fienberg, 1995, pp. 23–37, by permission of Allen and Unwin Pty Ltd.

Lorie K Harris: for "Saki, the Boy Hunter" from *Tlingit Tales, Potlatch and Totem Poles* by Lorie K Harris, 1993, pp. 13–19, by permission of Naturegraph Publishers Inc.

Terry Jones: for "Tom and the Dinosaur" from *Fantastic Stories* by Terry Jones, 1992, pp. 112–120, by permission of Pavalion Books.

Margaret Mahy: for "The Horrible Holiday Treasure Hunt" from *Stacks of Stories*, ed. Mary Hoffman, Hodder Children's Books Ltd, 1997, pp. 136–153, by permission of the Library Association.

Philippa Pearce: for "What the Neighbours Did" from *What the Neighbours Did and Other Stories* by Philippa Pearce, Viking Kestrel, 1972. Copyright © Philippa Pearce, 1972, by permission of Penguin Books Ltd.

James Reeves: for "Titus in Trouble" from *Titus Trouble* by James Reeves. Copyright © James Reeves, by permission of Laura Cecil Literary Agency on behalf of the James Reeves Estate.

ACKNOWLEDGEMENTS

Colin Thompson: for "The Creature from the Black Dustbin" from *The Haunted Staircase and Other Stories* by Colin Thompson, Hodder Children's Books, 1996, pp. 84–95, by permission of Hodder and Stoughton Ltd.

Martin Waddell: for "Little Obie and the Flood" from *Rock River Stories* by Martin Waddell, illustrated by Elsie Lennox, 1991, pp. 7–25. Copyright © Martin Waddell, 1991, by permission of Walker Books Ltd., London.

Ursula Moray Williams: for "A Picnic with the Aunts". Copyright © Ursula Moray Williams, by permission of Curtis Brown Ltd, London on behalf of the author.

Michael Wilson: for "The Short Cut" from *School Journal*, 3:1, 1994. Copyright © Michael Wilson, 1994, by permission of Learning Media Ltd and the author.

Every effort has been made to trace the copyright holders but where this has not been possible or where any error has been made the publishers will be pleased to make the necessary arrangement at the first opportunity.